At the Roots
of the Modern Novel

Literatura, język i kultura Japonii

Katarzyna Sonnenberg

At the Roots of the Modern Novel

A Comparative Reading
of Ihara Saikaku's *The Life of an Amorous Woman*
and Daniel Defoe's *Moll Flanders*

JAGIELLONIAN UNIVERSITY PRESS

Seria: **Literatura, język i kultura Japonii**

REVIEWER
dr hab. Romuald Huszcza, prof. UJ

COVER DESIGN
Marcin Bruchnalski

This publication was financed by the Institute of Oriental Studies, Faculty of Filology at the Jagiellonian University in Kraków

ISBN 978-83-233-3904-5

www.wuj.pl

Jagiellonian University Press
Editorial Offices: Michałowskiego 9/2, 31-126 Kraków
Phone: +48 12 663 23 81, +48 12 663 23 82, Fax: +48 12 663 23 83
Distribution: Phone: +48 12 631 01 97, Fax: +48 12 631 01 98
Cell Phone: + 48 506006 674, e-mail: sprzedaz@wuj.pl
Bank: PEKAO SA, IBAN PL 80 1240 4722 1111 0000 4856 3325

Acknowledgements

I would like to express my great appreciation to Professor Teresa Bela and Professor Marta Gibińska, who supported my first attempts at parallel reading of the works by Daniel Defoe and Ihara Saikaku during my studies in the Department of English Studies of the Jagiellonian University.

Look there at my heart, God, look there at my heart! which you had
mercy on in the depths of the abyss. Let it tell you now – *yes*, my
heart – what it was looking for in the pit: Why was I gratuitously evil?
Why was there no cause of my malice except malice? It was foul,
and I passionately wanted it. I loved it. I loved – I wanted – to perish!
I loved my own failing – not something I was failing *for* – but I loved
my own failing itself. My twisted soul was plunging from your solid
ground into outer chaos, hungering – not for something disgraceful,
but for disgrace.

(St. Augustine's Confessions II, 4, 9)

But I have a theory of my own about what this art of the novel is, and
how it came into being. To begin with, it does not simply consist in the
author's telling a story about the adventures of some other person. On
the contrary, it happens because the storyteller's own experience of
men and things, whether for good or ill – not only what he has passed
through himself, but even events which he has only witnessed or been
told of – has moved him to an emotion so passionate that he can no
longer keep it shut up in his heart. Again and again something in his
own life or in that around him will seem to the writer so important
that he cannot bear to let it pass into oblivion. There must never come
a time, he feels, when men do not know about it. That is my view of
how this art arose.

(Murasaki Shikibu, Genji Monogatari, "Hotaru")

Contents

10

Prologue

In his famous *The Rise of the Novel* Ian Watt (1957) focuses on Daniel Defoe (1660–1731), Samuel Richardson (1689–1761) and Henry Fielding (1707–1764) as precursors of the novel, understood as a "literary vehicle of a culture which, in the last few centuries, has set an unprecedented value on originality, on the novel; and it is therefore well named" (13). John Richetti (2008b) also acknowledges the significance of Defoe as the "first truly modern English writer" (3). Novak (1996) refers to a widespread conviction that modern novel in England began in either 1719 with Daniel Defoe's *Robinson Crusoe* or in 1740 with Samuel Richardson's *Pamela* (41). These opinions are closely connected with the fact that Defoe significantly differed from his literary predecessors in his choice of the material he used and developed into plots. As a writer he seemed less interested in the stories known from mythology, historical accounts or earlier works of literature. He rather focused on his own times and the richness of themes and problems they had to offer.

Ihara Saikaku (1642–1693), a Japanese writer whose final years of artistic creativity concurred with the Genroku era (1688–1704), like Defoe, is commonly associated with the development of townsmen culture and new achievements in literature. Saikaku, remembered as a *tsūjin* or a connoisseur of his times, was responsible for establishing one of the most popular genres of fiction writing in Japan: *ukiyozōshi* or "the stories of the floating world,"[1] which belonged to the *gesaku bungaku* ("entertainment or playful literature")[2] tradition, with sex and money as two greatest interests (De Bary

---

[1] The previous transcription of *uki* in *ukiyo* which was a Buddhist concept of "this world of grief and sorrow" was replaced with the homonymous *uki* meaning "floating" or "passing."

[2] Hibbett argues that the word *gesaku bungaku*, or "playful writing", which denotes the whole range of Tokugawa popular fiction, may be found as a dictionary equivalent to the English words "burlesque" and "literary parody" (Hibbett 1957: 54). Fowler follows

et al. 2005: 314). Traganou notices the novelty of this genre characterised by "themes derived from contemporary everyday life" and claims that it "instituted a mode of writing based on non-literary and vernacular speech" (227).

Saikaku's writings belong to the early-modern narratives which later influenced the development of the modern novel and although the name of "the first modern novel" in Japan is most frequently attributed to Futabatei Shimei's (1864–1909) *Ukigumo* (*Floating Cloud*, 1887),[3] it is hard to imagine Futabatei's narration without the tradition of the Edo period *gesaku bungaku* and Ihara Saikaku as its great representative.[4]

The significance of Saikaku to modern Japanese novelists may be seen in the fact that the development of the modern novel in Meiji period (1868–1912) corresponded with the rediscovery of Saikaku's writings in the 1880s (Kornicki 1998: 467). The first criticism devoted to Saikaku and his works comes from the end of the nineteenth century (Morris 1963: 49–51). Kōda Rohan, Mori Ōgai, and Ozaki Kōyō were among those who showed a keen interest in the author of *The Life of an Amorous Woman* (Lane 1955: 181–199; Teruoka 1957a 104–118). For some modern writers Saikaku was a symbol of Japanese literary tradition in prose and they referred to him in response to the inflow of European novels in Japan at the time. For others, however, he became a predecessor of the modern novel, praised for his realistic depiction of the lives of townspeople and the pleasure quarters. They were fascinated by the vivid depictions of the "daily life during his time in such accurate detail that even later Edo period historians used him to under-

---

Kitamura Tōkoku's distinction between "refined" and "vulgar" fiction and indicates that *gesaku bungaku* belonged to the latter: "Tokugawa literature had no lack of fiction. On the contrary, a great deal was being written in the form of *gesaku*, a generic term for such forms as the *kibyoshi* (illustrated "yellow-covered books"), *sharebon* ("sophisticated books" about the gay quarters), *kokkeibon* ("humorous books"), *ninjobon* ("amatory books"), and *yomihon* (didactic "reading books"). Its very name (literally, "playful composition"), however, suggested its "frivolous" and therefore non-literary character. *Gesaku* were often authored (usually anonymously) by samurai intellectuals, but their primary audience was the lower classes, mainly townspeople" (Fowler 1988: 24).

[3] Futabatei Shimei, *Japan's First Modern Novel: Ukigumo of Futabatei Shimei*, trans. Marleigh Grayer Ryan, New York, Columbia University Press 1965. Shimazaki Tōson's *Hakai* (*Broken Commandment*, 1906) is often regarded as a further development of Japanese modern novel: "Tayama Katai, and Tōson himself, the naturalists are celebrated as marking the successful culmination of the drive to develop a realistic modern novel in Japan" (Bourdaghs 2003: 109).

[4] As Fowler (1988) emphasizes, "Futabatei was influenced as much by his samurai lineage and Tokugawa heritage as by his studies of western literature" (25).

stand the past" (Chaiklin 2009: 47). This aspect of his writings is emphasised also nowadays in and outside Japan and Saikaku's "realistic picture of the contemporary world" is praised for providing important insights into Japanese history and culture (Nishiyama 1997: 199).[5]

This monograph brings together two works, one written by Ihara Saikaku, the seventeenth-century Japanese author, and another by Daniel Defoe, the journalist and novelist of Augustan England.[6] Although *Kōshoku Ichidai Onna* (*The Life of an Amorous Woman*, 1686)[7] and *Moll Flanders* (1722)[8] belong to different cultures and traditions, they are considered important steps in the formation of a new mode of writing in Japan and England respectively. The correspondences between the themes of the two works led Howard Hibbett (1957), who read Saikaku's novel within the convention of burlesque, to praise *The Life of an Amorous Woman* as "more artistic and more sensational" (64) than *Moll Flanders*, far too moralising for Hibbett's taste. The narrators of the two texts are different, as is their situation within the narrative; however, a parallel reading of *The Life of an Amorous Woman* and *Moll Flanders* does not always have to be so contradistinctive and harsh towards Defoe. To prove this Machiko M. Willey (2004) juxtaposed the two authors as social critics of their times.

The approach in this monograph differs from the previous ones as it focuses on the mode of confession and its possible contribution to the narration of the novels by Saikaku and Defoe. Although "confession" is understood here above all as "the act of revealing," traditional connotations and associations with the word are also considered. The comparative reading explores the tradition of confession in England and Japan, as well as its conventions and unavoidable paradoxes involved in using confession as a narrative strategy in a work of fiction. Although chronologically Saikaku preceded Defoe,

---

[5] Iwona Kordzińska-Nawrocka (2010) also admits that Saikaku was truly "the greatest realist of his era" (288).

[6] The term is used here with reference to the culture, as well as literary and social conventions in the century after the restoration of the English monarchy under Charles II in 1660.

[7] In this monograph the quotations come from Ivan Morris' translation and the title is shortened to "AM."

[8] Full title: "The Fortunes and Misfortunes of the Famous Moll Flanders, Etc. Who was born in Newgate, and during a life of continu'd Variety for Threescore Years, besides her Childhood, was Twelve Year a *Whore*, five times a *Wife* (whereof once to her own brother), Twelve Year a *Thief*, Eight Year a Transported *Felon* in *Virginia*, at last grew *Rich*, liv'd *Honest* and died a *Penitent*. Written from her own Memorandums." When quoted in this monograph referred to as "MF."

due to the distance in time and space, as well as to the historical and cultural circumstances, there is no possible direct influence of the former writer on the latter. Therefore, the chronological order will not always be kept in this book, especially in the first part of the chapter on the development of the novel.

Chapter I. The Development of the Novel

I.1. Narratives in Prose in Defoe's England and Saikaku's Japan

Defoe's England and Saikaku's Japan were characterised by an increasing interest in books among common people who were frequently semiliterate and enjoyed popular stories. Watt records that in Defoe's times in London shop names replaced pictorial signs, which implies the growing possibility of written communication at the time (Watt 1957: 36). Although the level of and the access to popular schooling still left much space for improvement, the opportunities to learn how to read must have been available to a broader public.

In Japan, the Edo period (1600–1867) was a time when the publishing market flourished (first of all in the region of Kyoto and Osaka – known as Kamigata, then in Edo) to the extent that some publishers began to specialise in certain types of books to cater to the needs of a given group of readers.[9] Kazuko Hioki estimates that towards the end of the Edo period more than half of the population in Japan were literate (Hioki 2009: 23). The highest rate of literacy could be noted among samurai, however by the mid-eighteenth century schooling became available also to townspeople in *terakoya* or temple schools (Kornicki 1998: 258). The education also spread among the rural elite, giving rise to *chihō bunjin* or "provincial literati who could have been of samurai or of merchant origins" (Rubinger 2007: 62).

The rise of literacy noticeable in Saikaku's Japan and Defoe's England was encouraged by the expansion of print. However, in Saikaku's time most of the *chōnin* still "had no more than the basic education" offered by *terakoya* and not many were truly able to read works such as *The Life of an Am-*

---

[9] Laura Moretti (2012) researches the catalogues and explores the history of the Edo-period publishers (199–308).

16

orous Woman (Katō 1997: 161). Still, in Defoe's England and in Saikaku's Japan alike, the circulating libraries enabled a great number of people to read popular books of all types, including novels and illustrated stories. With the development of the merchants' culture, the expensive woodblock-printing methods could also be used on a broader scale in Japan (Lane 1957: 644).

The development and popularisation of print influenced the style of reading marked by "the isolation and self-enclosure of the silent reader" (Richetti 1996: 7). Moreover, the situation of the publishing industries and growing literacy must have influenced the production of literature. A growing number of people could read and Saikaku was surely not the only one to believe that "there is nothing more shameful than being illiterate" (Dore 1984: 20). There was an increasing demand for books, which opened the space for a number of popular writers in England and Japan, including Defoe and Saikaku.

These were the circumstances in which the modern novel was born. It used the dynamics of the book market, focused on current themes and problems but it also was related to the already-existing literary genres. In the English tradition, the distinction between a romance and a novel has long remained the subject of debate. William Congreve in his preface to *Incognita* (1692) wrote about the differentiation between romances, which are "generally composed of the constant loves and invincible courage of heroes, heroines, kings and queens, mortals of the first rank, and so forth" and novels, which are of a "more familiar nature" (10). Similarly, Walter Scott distinguished between the "marvellous and uncommon incidents" in romances as opposed to "ordinary train of human events, and the modern state of society" (*ibid.*). The modern novel may thus be said to break with traditional themes and forms, which is noticeable also in the modern novelists' choice of names for the characters in their works. Names full of literary connotations were gradually replaced by such which would sound more contemporary or plausible (Watt 1957: 19).

In Japan, as Fowler notices in his book on *shishōsetsu*, the origin of fiction lay in vivid observation of reality and the influence of other literary genres was conspicuous:

> [T]he starting point in much Japanese "fiction" has not been the construction of a hypothetical situation but the observation of an actual one. This modus operandi is hardly unique to the *shishosetsu*; precedents can be found in such classical forms as the *zuihitsu* (discursive essay), *kana nikki* (poetic diary), *haibun* (haiku and prose), and *kikobun* (travel sketches), all of which are literary descriptions of lived experience (Fowler 1988: 17).

Fowler emphasises how narratives in Japan were exceptionally open and embracing all possible influences:

> The presentational mode infuses not only *waka, haikai*, and other poetic forms but also such prose forms as the "fictional tale" (*tsukuri monogatari*), "poem tale" (*uta monogatari*), "story of the 'floating world'" (*ukiyo zoshi*), "poetic diary" (*kana nikki*), and discursive essay (*zuihitsu*), to name the most prominent examples (Fowler 1988: 21).[10]

The influence of the tradition of *nikki* in Japan on the novel and the problem of realism will be addressed later on in this book. Here, it is important to emphasise that the Japanese modern novel was influenced not only by *nikki*, *kikōbun* and *haibun* but also by *ukiyozōshi*, which were preceded by a rich and heterogeneous tradition of *monogatari* – prose narratives sometimes compared to epic, highly conventional in character. The *monogatari* were additionally shaped by "the highly conventionalized aesthetics of the native verse forms and the nondramatic historiography of Chinese chronicles" (19).

The first example of vernacular fiction belonging to the *monogatari* tradition in Japan may be found as early as the tenth century. *Taketori Monogatari* (*The Tales of the Bamboo Cutter*, ca. 909) and *Ise Monogatari* (*The Tales of Ise*, ca. 947) are the earliest examples: the former may be considered a folktale, while the latter is a collection of short narratives and accompanying poems centred around an idealised character traditionally identified with Ariwara no Narihira. These two *monogatari* were later quoted and evoked by other writers, thus contributing to the conventionalisation of the genre, which reached its fullest development in the eleventh century when Murasaki Shikibu wrote *Genji Monogatari* (*The Tale of Genji*), depicting life in the imperial court during the Heian period and creating a male character who epitomised beauty, sensibility and elegance. The term *monogatari* was so deeply rooted in Japanese tradition and so intricately connected with fictional narratives that some modern novels in foreign languages were even translated into Japanese as *monogatari*.

---

[10] Fowler also notices that the various literary genres and modes were unified by the use of corresponding literary tropes and figures: "the familiar vocabulary of pivot words (*kakekotoba*), prefaces (jo), epithets (*makura kotoba*), association words (*engo*), and poetic place-names (*uta makura*) (...) for many centuries had provided a context for meaning and had made such ostensibly 'personal' genres as the *zuihitsu* and *kana nikki* both highly conventional and more accessible to their audience..." (Fowler 1988: 18).

Ukiyozōshi, much indebted to the medieval *otogizōshi* (fairytales and adventure stories which were often recited and then written in illustrated scrolls), were distinguished from *monogatari* with regards to their form – they were printed – and their content. They depicted the "floating world" (*ukiyo*) of pleasures and sorrows experienced by townspeople of the time. Even if they did not reject the previous motifs and patterns altogether, they used parody, which was an important stage in the development of the novel not only in Japan.

It is possible to say that in contrast with romances or *monogatari* (and also *otogizōshi*), which frequently explored the unfamiliar themes and evoked traditional imagery, *ukiyozōshi*, which belonged to the tradition of popular stories written in *kana* syllabary or *kanazōshi*, reflected the "here and now" of the writers and thus distanced themselves from the already existing conventions.

It is assumed that the break with the previous conventions which occured in modern novels corresponded with the writers' desire to depict the outside world. The juxtaposition is well captured by Watt (1957): "[t]he previous stylistic tradition for fiction was not primarily concerned with the correspondence of words to things, but rather with the extrinsic beauties which could be bestowed upon description and action by the use of rhetoric" (28). The shift from the language of description to the described object is therefore one characteristic of the modern novel. The strong connection between the novel and the outer world is visible also in the use of news and gossip in the narratives. Lennard Davis (1996) even argues that the novel was born as a response to the eagerness with which readers waited for news and wanted to read about the actual events and ordinary people (50). These expectations were answered both by Defoe and Saikaku.

Defoe used the news and gossip accessible at the time to develop his plots. Charles Lamb in his *Letter to Walter Wilson* (1822) noticed this dependence on external sources saying: "It is like reading evidence in a court of Justice" (Watt 1957: 34). Saikaku was also dependent on the gossip (*hanashi* or *uwasa*) and current news in his writings, which – according to Katō Shūichi (1980) – enabled him to write vividly and reliably (109–114). However, he was always creative in his use of facts (Teruoka 1957b: 375–394). The reader's eagerness to know the truth was thus played with in his narratives.

I.2. Realism and the Novel

Although examining the development of the novel through the lens of realism is debatable and much limiting, in the case of this monograph it is not entirely unjustified or fruitless. On the one hand, James Fujii (1993), following Masao Miyoshi, understandably opposes the views that the Japanese modern novel is characterised by "an extended attempt to appropriate conventions of the nineteenth century European realist novel, particularly a novel built around an individual subject" (2). Such Eurocentric views result in presenting Japanese literature as distant and frequently deficient in standards imposed by European writers and critics. On the other hand, the realistic representation of places, people and events indicating an intimate (even if inevitably arbitrary) relation between the narrated world and the outer reality remains one characteristic which distinguishes the novel from other fictional works written before. Here is how Warner summarises the tendency:

> The idea that the novel effects a particularly compelling imitation of "real life" is as old as seventeenth-century critical claims on behalf of the novella against the romance. (…) To represent "real" life is to attain a more valuable species of writing. Making this claim on behalf of the novel and against romance was a way critics promoted the surpassing of the old romance, with its fabulous elements and its extravagant codes of honor, in favor of a rational modern taste in entertainment (Warner 2011: 230).

The definition of "realism" is far from unambiguous even in Europe, where it is frequently analysed in the context of Western philosophy and said to reflect the characteristics of the modern period in its tendency to separate itself from the previous traditions and focus on the particular rather than the universal. The novel thus reflected the tendencies of the time in which it developed, focusing on the specific and the individual (Aaron 1952: 18–41). Moreover, since René Descartes' *Cogito Argument* refolmulated the problem of universals as a problem of a dualism between *ego* and the external world (Watt 1957: 294–295), modern novelists also started to oscillate between the individual and the external reality.

Daniel Defoe, who was known to have "the accuracy of finish of a Dutch painter… content to produce effects by the patient labour of minuteness" (Watt 1957: 17), with a commitment resembling that of Rebrandt, explored the reality of the concrete. It is worth noticing here that it was Rembrandt's work which was first described as "realistic" in 1835 in opposition to the neo-classical paintings (Weinberg 1937: 114). Watt argues, however, that in the context of the modern novel, the term "realism" does not only mean depicting life from "the seamy side," but it also means portraying "all the varieties of human experience" (Watt 1957: 11). Such a realistic portrayal is visible in Defoe's works which focus on the individuals "as they examine the conditions of their existence and explore what it means to be a person in particularized social and historical circumstances" (Richetti 2008a: 121).

The emphasis on the individualinevitably results in introducing a number of uncertainties into the description of reality. Defoe's technique of writing embraces the uncertainties and is referred to by Ian Watt (1957) as a "formal realism," defined as "the premise, or primary convention, that the novel is a full and authentic report of human experience, and therefore under an obligation to satisfy its reader with such details of the story as the individuality of the actors concerned, the particulars of the times and places of their actions, [and] details which are presented through a more largely referential use of language than is common in other literary forms" (32). Accordingly, the reliability of characters who are not mere types, but individualised beings, and the use of concrete objects, places and dates shape Defoe's realistic narration.

The use of the term "realism" is even more problematic in Japan where it is associated with the urge to impose on Japanese literature the dictates of European artists and writers (Fujii 1993: 2). The term, translated as *shajitsu*, became popular – also due to Tsubouchi Shōyō's *Shōsetsu Shinzui* (The Essence of the Novel, 1885–1886) – as late as the nineteenth century and implied "sketching or copying" reality (Miller 2009: 103). Tsubouchi used it in opposition to the description complying with the imperative of *kanzen chōaku* ("the encouragement of virtue and the chastisement of vice") present in Edo period fiction.

It is not surprising that the Japanese term "realism" is strongly associated with the influences of Western literature in Meiji era, which shaped Shōyō's opinions on literature, and the two traditions of writing are often contrasted: "Whereas prose in the west, whether 'history' or 'fiction,' has been inextricably tied to the emplotted narrative, the Japanese have been more at home with literary forms that tend to undermine or circumvent the narrative flow" (Fowler 1988: 21). Fowler argues that while the western narratives traditionally focused on representation and used plausible plots, in Japan it was the "presentational mode" that prevailed:

> In the absence of a highly representational mode, the influence of a more self-consciously presentational mode on Japanese fiction has been enormous. The latter mode has played no small role in western literature as well – as the continuing interest in tropes, for example, demonstrates – but it has not had the sweeping impact, especially on prose, that it has had on Japanese literature (Fowler 1988: 20–21).

The "representational mode" in Japanese fiction is thus considered a product of westernization. This opinion, however, may be questioned in the view of the fact that Meiji writers in their search for representational techniques turned to Ihara Saikaku. Such novelists as Shimamura Hōgetsu, Tayama Katai and Masamune Hakuchō, who were fascinated by Western naturalistic description, eagerly emphasised Saikaku's realism.[11] The term "realism," was of course applied to Saikaku's works *a posteriori* (Hiroshima 1993: 153–154). Moreover, for the Japanese writers the realistic representation of "here and now" did not necessarily exclude elements of idealisation and stylisation, commonly regarded as useful means leading to a convincing representation of reality (Keene 2001: 89–109). Therefore Saikaku's literature was readily interpreted in the context of realism, despite its use of supernatural elements, frequent stylisations and idealization of the characters. Sometimes, to distinguish it from Western tradition, Saikaku's writing method was referred to as the Edo-period realism (or Tokugawa realism – from the name of the ruling shogun dynasty).

The realistic qualities of Saikaku's writings are enumerated by Berry:

> Saikaku's fiction is a close cousin of the texts of the information library. It, too, focuses on a contemporary and mundane world – the commonplace here and now of readers. And it, too, observes that world with what appears an empirical exactness. The action of the tales may flout routine, but Saikaku locates his drama in thick physical settings that convey a sense of realism. He names real names, from temples to castles, from urban wards to individual firms (Berry 2006: 214).

With its focus on real names and settings, Saikaku's manner of depiction contributed to the "change in literature, toward closer integration into a cultivated, thriving, commercial society" (Hibbett 1952: 418).

As one of the requirements of realism in fiction is its focus on the individual, the use of the first-person perspective should also be considered an important realistic strategy and – since the identity of the first-person narrators is established in relation to their past experiences – the plot is sustained

---

[11] In 1901 Shimamura published his article "Saikaku ron" on Saikaku's *kōshoku mono* (erotic stories) in *Fūunshū* (Shimamura 1975: 1–38).

by their credibility. The individual experience thus becomes the core of the novel. Defoe's use of the first-person narratives reflects the seventeenth-century change in the philosophical perspective: "total subordination of the plot to the pattern of the autobiographical memoir is as defiant an assertion of the primacy of individual experience in the novel as Descartes's *cogito ergo sum* was in philosophy" (Watt 1957: 14). By exploiting memoirs, diaries or letters in his novels and presenting them as truly existing Defoe proved his acceptance of the "primacy of individual experience." This characteristic use of autobiographical mode is described by Richetti:

> Despite this variegated nature of experience, this relativity of the "real" that they dramatize, Defoe's narratives claim aggressively to be literally true. They are fake autobiographies, life stories of supposedly actual people. These claims, doubtless, tell us what Defoe thought his readers wanted. Like all his subsequent fictions, Robinson Crusoe (1719) features a title page advertising the memoirs of a "real" person (Richetti 1975: 123).

Defoe insisted on the truthfulness of his accounts. Robinson Crusoe, Moll Flanders and Roxana may all be fictional characters but they are introduced as real people in order to appeal to the modern readers, and the novels include crucial elements of confession which validate the accounts and create an intimate relationship between the narrator and the reader.

Contrary to Defoe, Saikaku does not insist that the accounts presented in his *ukiyozōshi* are true. Neither are his characters developed in a sustained manner. They are often flat, resembling rather types than actual human beings, which may be related to the burlesque quality of Saikaku's writings and to its comic tone (Hibbett 1957: 59). This tone, present also in Saikaku's poetic works (*haikai*), which preceded his prose, enabled social criticism and provided entertainment at the same time. It also constituted a connection between the story and the cultural and social milieu of Edo Japan.

Despite his tendency to shift narrative perspectives in other works, in *The Life of an Amorous Woman* Saikaku introduces the first-person narrator, a woman who reflects on her past in a form of a confession addressed at those who are willing to listen. This may be a burlesque on a Buddhist confessional tale (also used in later novels, e.g. Ozaki Kōyō' *Sannin bikuni irozange*, 1889, translated into English as *Repentance of the Two Nuns*), but it is also a narrative strategy devised in response to the reader's possible expectations. Rimer (1978) rightly indicates the long-existing tradition of "the false I" in Japanese literary tradition (80). However, it is also possible to suggest a noticeable connection between the development of the modern novel and the first-person narration written in a mode of confession, even if it is used in a burlesque manner. The complex relationship between realism and confession in fiction will be analysed in more detail in Chapter III.

I.3. Towards a Modern Novel

Abel Chevalley in *The Modern English Novel* indicates an unavoidable difficulty in defining the genre and its origin:

> It is difficult to define the novel, and especially the English novel, because of its extreme plasticity. Only in mathematics can a given object be circumscribed with precision: whatever is not amenable to mathematical laws escapes scientific definition; and this is particularly true of that subjective image of the world of which literature, in its divers forms, is only an essayed transcription (1).

Chevalley attributes the difficulty to the plasticity and rich traditions of the English fiction writing. In Japan the situation is at least as much difficult. The rise of the modern novel is commonly associated with the transitions in language and narration which occurred in the Meiji era (1868–1912) under the influence of Western (mostly English, Russian, and French) literature. Nonetheless, the previous genres and modes of expression did not disappear but rather were explored and adapted to the new conditions. Katō Shūichi (1997) emphasises that "Japanese literature since the Meiji period has found new modes of expression either in western literature (…) or in Japan's own past" and he enumerates "*waka* and *haiku*, *zuihitsu*, certain types of novel" as examples of the traditional genres (265).

The relationship between the old and the new in modern Japanese novel is complex. With the arrival of a new era the new postulates to improve the old *gesaku* tradition of writing were formulated. The most representative and influential ones were gathered in Tsubouchi Shōyō's *Shōsetsu Shinzui*. Tsubouchi in his work recapitulates the rich tradition of prose in Japan, beginning with *Genji Monogatari*, and including Ihara Saikaku as a representative of a glorious Genroku period:

> What a glorious tradition the novel can boast in Japan! We have from ancient times such works as *The Tale of Genji*, and in more recent centuries Saikaku and other novelists have won considerable fame with their writings. The novel has enjoyed an

ever increasing popularity, and writers have eagerly turned out historical romances, humorous tales, or love stories, as their particular talents dictated. However, as the result of the upheavals which accompanied the Meiji Restoration, for a time the popular writers ceased their activity, and the novel itself consequently lost ground. It has only been recently that a revival has occurred (Tsubouchi 1960: 55).

Despite his comments on the "glorious past" of Japanese fiction, Tsubouchi notices, however, that the *gesaku* tradition "lost its ground" on the threshold of modernity. He blames the decline on the writers' eagerness to respond to their readers' lowest instincts:

> In actual practice, however, only stories of bloodthirsty cruelty or else of pornography are welcomed, and very few readers indeed even cast so much as a glance on works of a more serious nature. Moreover, since popular writers have no choice but to be devoid of self-respect and in all things slaves to public fancy and the lackeys of fashion, each one attempts to go to greater lengths than the last in pandering to the tastes of the time. They weave their brutal historical tales, string together their obscene romances, and yield to every passing vogue (Tsubouchi 1960: 57).

Tsubouchi's view that the attempt to respond to the demands of a broader audience gradually led to a decline in the art of fiction is shared by many and accepted also nowadays. As a consequence, Lane (1959) states that the writers after Saikaku "were not his equals, and as often as not the new forms were only extensions of some genre he had already created and explored" (137). With the dawn of modernity, *gesaku* writers became a popular target of criticism both for the lowly content and for the unsuitable language of their works:

> The pose of frivolousness struck by *gesaku* authors made their work the object of critical scorn in the Meiji period, but that judgement was based on the need of Meiji authors to distance themselves from the traditions of the past in order to define their own modern identity, and it does not take into account the historical and ideological contexts of late Tokugawa fiction. (Washburn 1995: 75).

Weak plots and descriptions of *gesaku* writings were commonly stigmatised in Meiji Japan. "These weaknesses – as Hijiya-Kirschnereit (1996) explains – were both the cause and the result of the low regard in which narrative literature was held by intellectuals" and it was Tsubouchi's insistence that "fiction was a self-relevant artistic genre" that eventually "led to major innovations in literature" (15).

The low regard of fiction was not something limited to Meiji Japan. The more popular fiction became in England, the more often its quality and significance was questioned. Warner (2011) remarks that "[d]uring the decades following 1700, a quantum leap in the number, variety, and popularity of novels led many to see novels as a catastrophe to book-centered culture" (226). "Novels," or new and secret stories by Aphra Behn, Delariviere Manley, and Eliza Haywood, were also added to the list of the books at which the anti-novel discourse was aimed. The authors were often accused of creating the "aura of sexual scandal," as well as of corrupting the morale of their readers. Warner indicates how they responded to the accusations:

> The debate about the dangers of novel reading changed the kind of novels that were written. First, cultural critics sketched the first profile of the culture-destroying pleasure-seeker who haunts the modern era: the obsessive, unrestrained consumer of fantasy. Novelists like Manley and Haywood included this figure of the pleasure-seeking reader within their novels, as a moral warning to their readers (...). Then, novelists like Richardson and Fielding, assuming the cogency of this critique, developed replacement fictions as a cure for the novel-addicted reader. In doing so, they aimed to deflect and reform, improve and justify novelistic entertainment (Warner 2011: 227).

Apparently, there were two attitudes the writers could take towards the accusation of corrupting their readers: either present the immoral behaviour with the declared aim to stigmatise it, or create a new type of fiction.

The situation was not too dissimilar in Japan. An attempt to respond to the accusations targeted at the writers of fiction is to be found already in *Genji Monogatari*, the famous 11th century work by Murasaki Shikibu. In the chapter entitled "Hotaru" ("Fireflies") Murasaki argues that writers, even at the risk of being criticised, cannot omit describing vices and follies:

> Clearly then, it is no part of the storyteller's craft to describe only what is good or beautiful. Sometimes, of course, virtue will be his theme, and he may then make such play with it as he will. But he is just as likely to have been struck by numerous examples of vice and folly in the world around him, and about them he has exactly the same feelings as about the pre-eminently good deeds which he encounters: they are important and must all be garnered in. Thus anything whatsoever may become the subject of a novel, provided only that it happens in this mundane life and not in some fairyland beyond our human ken (Murasaki 1960: 500).

Murasaki defends the romances which, she believes, are not merely "frivolous fabrications," and she also indicates that there will "always be a distinction between the lighter and the more serious forms of fiction"(502).

Murasaki's apology of fiction may have been convincing to some but it surely did not dismiss all the accusations since centuries later Ueda Akinari

(1734–1809) in the "Preface" to his *Ugetsu monogatari* (*Tales of Moonlight and Rain*, 1776) referred to Murasaki, albeit ironically, as "being condemned to hell":

> Lo Kuan-chung wrote *Water Margin*, and for three generations he begot deaf mutes. For writing *The Tale of Genji*, Lady Murasaki was condemned to hell. Thus were these authors punished for what they had done. But consider their achievement. Each created a rare form, capable of expressing all degrees of truth with infinitely subtle variation and causing a deep note to echo in the reader's sensibility wherewith one can find mirrored realities of a thousand years ago (Ueda 1974: 97).

Ueda Akinari, a writer of fiction himself, by emphasising the achievements of Murasaki and other authors, who expressed the subtlety and variety of truth through fiction, attempts to defend himself against impending accusations:

> By chance, I happened to have some idle tales with which to entertain you, and as they took shape and found expression, with crying pheasants and quarrelling dragons, the stories came to form a slipshod compilation. But you who pick up this book to read must by no means take the stories to be true. I hardly wish for my offspring to have hare lips or missing noses (Ueda 1974: 97).

Ueda, anticipating imminent allegations, in a humorous manner (in the last line he hyperbolically presents dramatic consequences his fiction might bring to his children and grandchildren) insists that his stories are not meant to be unquestionably true but that they belong to the tradition of "fabrications," as opposed to the highest forms of literature which, to use Fowler's description, "were public and utilitarian in orientation and meant to aid in the art of government" (1988: 22). Like in England, in Japan writers tried to defend the value of their works by including a moral message in accordance with *kanzen chōaku* imperative, but mostly they used the imperative as a pretext or camouflage against censorship. "Nevertheless they find it so difficult to abandon the pretext of 'encouraging virtue' that they stop at nothing to squeeze in a moral, thereby distorting the emotion portrayed, falsifying the situations, and making the whole plot nonsensical" – Tsubouchi deplores the state of affairs and comments harshly on such practices (57).

The inferior position of fiction in Edo period Japan corresponded with the situation in China. This is the context in which the Japanese term *shōsetsu*, used as a translation of the English term "novel," appeared:

> The bias against prose fiction was even stronger and also reflected Chinese literary tastes. The word for prose fiction itself (*shosetsu* [*hsiao-shuo* in Chinese] originally

meant "unofficial history" and referred to popular, loosely historical accounts written in the vernacular) is indicative of the low esteem in which it was held. *Shosetsu* might be translated literally as "small talk"; a *shosetsuka* was therefore someone who collected "street talk" and "roadside gossip" and committed them to writing (Fowler 1988: 23).

Shōsetsu, the term nowadays commonly used to embrace all types of narratives, such as novel, novella, short-story (with no restrictions regarding length), originally appeared in opposition to verse and was associated with common gossip. At the time when the "content of 'literature'" was poetry, serving "as a vehicle of expression," and nonfiction prose, which functioned "as the moral guideline for the literati class" (Fowler 1988: 22), *shōsetsu* was not highly evaluated

The reference to popular gossip in the name of the genre also suggests the ambiguity of truth in fiction. Fujii (1993) notices that "the boundary that separates it (*shōsetsu*) from other genres such as essays, meditations, diaries, and biographies is much less defined than it commonly is in the West" (14). This may be true with reference to the contemporary novel, but in the eighteenth century the division between fact and fiction was not a clear one also in England. By the nineteenth century the genre of the novel was already established, however the eighteenth century, of which Daniel Defoe is a great representative, was still the time of flux. Richetti (1996) defines it as follows:

> To read fiction from the early and even the middle years of the eighteenth century is to enter a narrative situation in which the boundaries between the ordinary and everyday world of fact and event (such as we now read about in newspapers and watch unfold on television) and the fictional or sensational or even fantastic realm are fluid and uncertain (1–2).

The situation of English novel in Defoe's times resembles in this respect that of the pre-Meiji narratives in Japan.

The ambiguity of the term *shōsetsu* usually translated into English as "novel" entails further complications expressed by Zwicker in a sequence of questions: "do we treat the *Genji* as a 'novel,' and thus begin the history of the Japanese novel in the eleventh century? Or is the *Genji* something else entirely? And if the *Genji* is a novel, then does that imply that the history of the novel as such also begins in Japan – and not in Europe?" (439).[12]

---

[12] Zwicker includes interesting comments on the reception of *Genji Monogatari* in the West: "When a partial translation appeared in the late nineteenth century, it seemed essentially

The answers to these questions are far from being obvious. Since the first systematic use of the term *shōsetsu* is noticed in Tsubouchi Shōyō's critical writings, researchers and critics tend to associate the term with Meiji literature.[13] It is true that with the new era and new challenges stemming from intensive contacts with the West Japanese novel had to develop not only new narrative strategies but also new vocabulary which would make it more valued.[14] Nonetheless, the questions regarding the relationship between *shō-setsu* and the earlier traditions of fiction remain unresolved. What leaves no doubt is that in their search for new ways of expression many modern writers explored Ihara Saikaku's *ukiyozōshi*, which speaks about the novelistic potential of the style and language of this Edo-period writer.

I.4. Saikaku and His Popular Fiction

Although Saikaku (1642–1693) is greatly appreciated for his brilliant portraits of his contemporaries and their times (e.g. in *Kōshoku Ichidai Otoko – The Life of an Amorous Man*; *Kōshoku Gonin Onna – Five Amorous Women*;

---

incomprehensible to Western readers: 'curious rather than interesting,' it was 'if not precisely impossible, then difficult to appreciate' (1898, 'Japanese Romance,' New York Times, 16 Apr.). Four decades on, however, the *Genji* was no longer so difficult to appreciate. In a 1938 review Jorge Luis Borges would describe the work as 'what one would quite precisely call a psychological novel' (187), arguing that such a novel would have been unthinkable in Europe before the nineteenth century. It was only with Arthur Waley's six-volume translation (1925–1933) that a framework would be found for comprehending the Genji not as a historical curiosity but as a peculiar form of the modern novel avant le lettre and as a masterpiece of world literature" (442–443).

[13] Tomi Suzuki notices: "Shōyō was the first to use the term shōsetsu systematically as a generic term for prose fiction in general. In the Tokugawa period, prose fiction was referred to by a variety of terms based on content – such as *ukiyo-zōshi* (books on the floating world), *sharebon* (books on the refined manners of the licensed quarters), and *ninjōbon* (books on human feelings) – or on physical appearance – such as *akahon* (red books, mainly illustrated books for children), *kurohon* (black books, historical fiction), *kibyōshi* (yellow books, illustrated humor and satire for adults) – or on the mode of presentation – such as *yomihon* (reading books) and *kusa-zōshi* (grass books, or illustrated books)" (Suzuki 1996: 20).

[14] "Unable to rely any longer on the 'worlds' and associations of classical literature or in any coherent way on an alien literary tradition, they began exploring the possibility of using their own lives as 'world.' Once the writer established his persona as a legitimate subject of literary discourse, he was working, as far as he and his audience were concerned, with familiar material and could allude to it in subsequent works in the knowledge that readers would be conversant with it" (Fowler 1988: 18).

Kōshoku Ichidai Onna – The Life of an Amorous Woman), his own life is not well known to modern readers. What little information is available comes from Itō Baiu's *Kenbun Dansō* (*Various Stories Heard and Seen*) dating back to 1738:

> [T]here was a townsman named Hirayama Tōgo in Osaka of Settsu Province. He was well-to-do, but his wife died early, and his only child, a blind daughter, also died. He turned over his business as a shop-clerk and lived exactly as he pleased, though he never became a priest. He would wander for about half the year all over the country, a wallet slung around his neck, like a pilgrim, then return home. He was extremely fond of haikai and studied with Isshō. Later he founded his own school. He changed his name to Saikaku and wrote such works as *Eitaigura, Nishi no umi,* and *Sejō Shimin Hinagata* (Keene 1999: 174).

Baiu's record provides scant but invaluable information about the author of *The Life of an Amorous Woman*. We learn that Saikaku (most probably Hirayama Tōgo's pen-name) came from the region of Osaka, renowned for its thriving trade as well as for the colourful culture of the townspeople. The passage makes clear that the merchants' ways of life were familiar to Saikaku, who worked for some time as a shop-clerk. It also discloses that both his wife and his daughter died, which must have affected Saikaku's life and career greatly. As Kengi Hamada (1964) comments upon Baiu's remark: "The tragedy moved him (Saikaku) so deeply that he turned over his business to his manager and led the life of a roving Buddhist monk. He travelled extensively, returning to Osaka once every six months or so" (6). Finally, the passage emphasises Saikaku's interest in the linked poems known as *haikai no renga*.

All of the information in Baiu's brief passage is highly relevant to the interpretation of Saikaku's works. Indeed, before he started writing prose, he was a prolific writer of *haikai,* appreciated by his readers and peers alike as simultaneously humorous and eccentric.[15] While being undeniably inspired by Japanese poetic tradition, Saikaku also rebelled against its refinement and against the strict requirements for stylistic and thematic purity. As a consequence, his poems are frequently considered lowbrow, inelegant, frivolous or even obscene. Their eccentricity and unconventionality resulted in their being referred to as written in "Dutch style" or *Ōranda ryū*.[16]

---

[15] According to tradition, Saikaku was to write "as many as 23,500 verses in a single day and night" (Stubbs 1965: 10).

[16] The interpretation of Saikaku's poetic style is given by Yamashita (1966) and Ogata (1957).

When Saikaku started writing in prose he frequently used the techniques he had previously mastered while writing poetry. His narratives are, therefore, characterised by numerous elisions, as well as allusions to distinguished works of literature. The meaning of his stories is more than once enriched by *engo* ("associated words") – two or more words related in meaning which were used in poetry, or *kakekotoba* ("pivot words") combining two or more ideas on the basis of homonymous similarity between words or phrases. In his narratives Saikaku used the mixture of the refined and the vulgar styles, a technique which in Meiji period was referred to as *gazoku set'chū* (a mixture of classical and colloquial languages) and was applied in a number of the novels written at the time. His language abounds in ellipses, juxtapositions and parallels and is influenced both by his experience as a *haikai* poet and by the colloquial language of his times (Mori 1969: 173–180; Fujimoto 1999: 28–37).

If the style and language of Saikaku's narratives are not too dissimilar from his poems, neither are the themes and motifs he employs. Both in poetry and in prose he is primarily interested in what may be considered coarse and scandalous but nonetheless constitutes a crucial part of human life and as such inevitably attracts the readers' attention. As Richard Lane (1973) indicates, Saikaku tells and retells "the adventures of gallants and rakes, of courtesans and harlots, of samurai and plebeian pederasts" (233). The themes of Saikaku's narratives are therefore deeply rooted in his experiences as a townsman and he was, in this respect, a good representative of his age – an age in which "the townspeople, who could boast of neither rank nor birth," could nonetheless "come to hold the hegemony of literary activities" (Stubbs 1965: 7).

Ihara Saikaku's works are commonly divided into three thematic groups: *kōshoku mono* ("the erotic things") focussing on the lives of mostly courtesans or actors of the *kabuki* theatre and on the pleasures the red-light districts offered to men in seventeenth-century Japan; *chōnin mono* ("the merchants' things") centred around the delights and, above all, the hardships of the merchants; finally, *buke mono* ("the warriors' things") depicting the customs and adventures of the samurai. The transition from *kōshoku mono* to other works is thus explained by Totman (1995):

> From about 1687 on, however, perhaps because the market for erotic tales was sated, Saikaku shifted to other topics. In works that profoundly enriched the genre and gave it most of its enduring value as a window on the age, he produced collections of tales exemplifying unfilial behavior, the principles of merchant conduct,

vendettas among samurai, and the samurai ethic of duty. Other writings treated bizarre tastes and interests, judicial decisions of the bakufu's administrator in Kyoto, incidents involving actors, the hardships of debtors, and the difficulty of getting ahead in life (215).

It is true that Saikaku's shift to other topics is noticeable but he continued to write *kōshoku mono* throughout his life.

Kōshoku Ichidai Onna (*The Life of an Amorous Woman*, 1686), the work analysed in this monograph, belongs to the first group. *Nippon Eitaigura* (*The Japanese Family Storehouse*, 1688) and *Seken Munezan'yō* (*The Scheming World*, 1692), from the second group, are the prominent examples of how Saikaku vividly depicted the lives of the merchants while conveying his clear didactic message. Finally, *Budō Denraiki* (*The Transmission of the Martial Arts*, 1687) and *Buke Giri Monogatari* (*Tales of Samurai Duty*, 1688) are works exploring the complexities of the lives of the samurai, often questioning the popular myths of the warriors' glorious revenge and of their moral conduct.

Kōshoku Ichidai Onna was preceded by another "erotic story," entitled *Kōshoku Ichidai Otoko* (*The Life of an Amorous Man*, 1682) which in fifty-four chapters vividly renders the sexually suggestive story of Yonosuke, a man representative of *ukiyo*: the "floating world" or the world of "transient pleasures" (Hibbett 1959 3). Noriko Kamachi (1999) summarises the protagonist's innumerable adventures to emphasise the scale of his erotic activities: "between the ages of 7 and 60, Yonosuke is said to have dallied with 3,742 women and frolicked with 725 boys" (59). The book, however, also provides the readers with "superb character sketches of the women he dallies with" (Hamada 1964: 7). It beautifully depicts the liveliness and excitement of the amusements awaiting men in seventeenth-century Japan.

Shortly before *The Life of an Amorous Woman* Saikaku also published *Kōshoku Gonin Onna* (*Five Women Who Loved Love*, 1685), yet another story describing the erotic adventures of its protagonists. This time, he depicted the lives and desires not of famous courtesans but of common girls living in the Edo-period towns or in the countryside. Although his collection of five independent stories may be deficient in psychological insight into the motives and true desires of the heroines, it is nonetheless an interesting attempt to render a woman's perspective on the narrated events.

I.5. Defoe and His Writings

Daniel Foe (1660–1731), as he was called for the first forty years of his life, is known for both his pamphlets and works of fiction.[17] He was a most versatile writer who tried his hand "at verse satire and prose satire, at political and religious controversy, at history, at journalism, at the essay, at the ode and the hymn and the panegyric, at straightforward narrative and semi-fictitious narrative" (Sutherland 1938: 227). In fact, he began his career as a journalist and, as Novak (1996) emphasises, "[h]e could charge a description of a battle such as Blenheim with a sense of action and movement lacking in accounts in other journals, and his *Review* was filled with illustrative stories and short allegories" (42). Rendering his name more aristocratic by adding the "De" may be indicative of his social aspirations and of artistic self-creation. In this respect, his change of name may be compared to Saikaku's taking a nom de plume.

Defoe's private life was intertwined with public history and its great events. In 1664, only about four years after his birth, London was attacked by the Dutch fleet. In 1665 the city's population was severely decimated by the plague and only one year later it was devastated by the Great Fire. It is uncertain whether or not Defoe could have had any recollection of the pestilence. Nonetheless, he depicted it in great detail in *A Journal of the Plague Year* (1722), the work which proves Defoe to be "a great journalist," who could "give a vivid picture of anything, whether he had seen it or not" (Sutherland 1938: 6). In fact, *A Journal of the Plague Year* might have been inspired by the diaries written by Henry Foe, Daniel Defoe's uncle and the work may certainly be said to have contributed to interpreting Defoe as a great realistic author, one whose writing is rooted in the external world.

If public history provided Defoe with inspiration as far as the themes of his writings are concerned, his private experiences shaped the ways he perceived what he depicted. In reading his works it is also important to consider Defoe's life story: he was brought up in a religious family, his parents were Presbyterian Dissenters and he himself was educated in the academy in Newington Green run by the Reverend Charles Morton.[18]

---

[17] The date of Defoe's birth is uncertain. Sutherland claims that 1660 is most likely (Sutherland 1938: 2).

[18] Sutherland emphasises the impact Charles Morton had on young Defoe – not only in his religious preaching but also in the style and language he used in writing (Sutherland 1938: 20).

Defoe's religious education and his convictions influenced what he wrote, be it his political pamphlets or works of fiction such as *Robinson Crusoe*, *Roxana* or *Moll Flanders*, where man is ultimately responsible before God for his conduct. As Novak (1963) realises, "God is always present in Defoe's works" (3). God is the beginning and the end of all things: "If any of Defoe's fictional characters falls into difficulties, Defoe will present a variety of natural causes to explain the situation, but the final cause is God" (Novak 1963: 7). The role of Creator in the world of Defoe's literature is of utmost importance.

It seems that his education in Newington Green also – if indirectly – affected Defoe's style of writing. As a young boy Defoe was acquainted with Greek and Latin but his knowledge was merely superficial. He believed – contrary to what he was taught – that it was English that should be studied and polished at school. He even complained at one point that the graduates of Newington Green were "critics in the Greek and Hebrew, perfect in languages, and perfectly ignorant, if that term may be allowed, of their mother-tongue" (*The Present State of Parties* 1712: 317; Sutherland 1938: 24). As a consequence, Defoe frequently emphasised the role of conversation in mastering English and shaping one's style in writing: "easy, free, plain, unaffected, and untainted with force, stiffness, formality, affected hard words, and all the ridiculous parts of a learned pedant" (*The Present State of Parties* 1712: 317; Sutherland 1938: 24).

Defoe was greatly influenced by his religious education and Christian ideals. Defying the expectations of some, he did not become a minister but chose a career in business, although Christianity always remained important to him. As a merchant, however, he was also affected by the experience he gained at his trade. In this respect, he resembles to a large degree the author of *The Life of an Amorous Woman*, a merchant who later in his life started writing stories about townspeople and samurai. Indeed, both Defoe and Saikaku truly could be called children of their times, focusing on what Rogers (1972) in his study of Defoe calls the "diversity of circumstances" (62). The writers' professional backgrounds prove to be the root cause of their pragmatism. In Defoe's case, living by his wits made him both respectful of and fascinated by the skills and craft of others, as reflected in the passages vividly describing Moll's resourcefulness or Captain Singleton's cunning, despite their professions of thievery and piracy being disreputable, and even atrocious.

What distinguishes Defoe from Saikaku is his involvement in political and social matters. As Dobrée rightly notices, Defoe was "politically minded" (Dobrée 1959: 36). Most of the time, he uses his pen to support the Whig stand. In his pamphlets collected in the volume *An Essay upon Projects* published in 1697, he overtly expresses his ideas on how to improve the economic and social situation in England. In "The Poor Man's Plea" he disapproves of discrimination against the poor inscribed in law and the criminal justice system. In the poem "The True-Born Englishman" (1701) he defends the position of King William III against his enemies, emphasising that the English derive from the Picts, the Normans, and the Danes among others, making it difficult to speak about either an English race or English gentility.

Defoe was even prosecuted for his political convictions. In 1702 he published his famous pamphlet "The Shortest Way with the Dissenters," in which he satirises the High Church Tories, pointing out the means available to readily exterminate the Protestant Dissenters. In response to this grim satire, which in tone resembles Jonathan Swift's "A Modest Proposal," Defoe was arrested, pilloried for three days and then taken to Newgate. The time spent in prison most probably influenced his views on criminals and punishment and almost certainly coloured his depiction of Newgate in *Moll Flanders*.

Defoe is recognised nowadays for his political treatises, but he is even more famous for his works of fiction. *Robinson Crusoe*, the story of a castaway first published in 1719, has held the interest of readers and publishers alike for nearly three hundred years.[19] His other semi-fictional or fictional writings also captivated readers by means of engrossing plots and simple style. *Captain Singleton* (1720) presents the life of an Englishman raised by Gipsies who goes on to become a skilful pirate travelling to distant lands. *Colonel Jack* (1722), on the other hand, resembles *Moll Flanders* (1722) as a story of a man's conversion and dreams of gentility. *Roxana: the Fortunate Mistress* (1724) focuses, as *Moll Flanders* does, on the lot of women who refused to comply with the requirements of society in mid-eighteenth-century England, and whose choice of profession was limited to either prostitution (Roxana's case) or thievery (Moll).

---

[19] *Robinson Crusoe* was one of the first European novels translated into Japanese. The translation by Kuroda Kikuro from the Dutch edition appeared in 1848.

I.6. *The Life of an Amorous Woman* and *Moll Flanders*

A comparative approach to Saikaku's and Defoe's lives reveals a number of similarities between two authors who lived and created in two different cultures.[20] They were both involved in trade and observed with due attention the customs and behaviour of merchants, while being fascinated by their craft and artistry. Both were highly prolific writers employing various techniques within diverse literary genres. While Saikaku explored the poetic technique of *haikai no renga* in his narratives, Defoe frequently resorted to the journalistic style while writing fiction.

However, it is not the biographical correspondences between Saikaku's and Defoe's lives but the similarities between their works, *The Life of an Amorous Woman* and *Moll Flanders*, which are the object of analysis in this monograph. The works were juxtaposed on the basis of their potential social criticism by Machiko Willey (2004). Hibbett (1993) also compares the two titles, emphasising that "the themes of the two works are similar," but "their narrative techniques differ" (62). Hibbett's view may be called into question, however, if we focus on the use of confessional mode in Saikaku's *The life of an Amorous Woman* and Defoe's *Moll Flanders*.

On the level of plot, both Saikaku and Defoe tell a story of a woman who wanted to pursue her dream and gradually descended "the scale of women's life" falling "to the lowest trade" (Seigle 1993: 182). Both the Amorous Woman and Moll are presented as outcasts, wilful and determined. The former is an illegitimate child of a minor noble, the latter a daughter of a thief.

On the level of themes, however, contrary to what Hibbett claims, the two works differ conspicuously. *The Life of an Amorous Woman* focuses on sexual desire and sensuous pleasure. The first-person protagonist indulges in her erotic adventures told and retold to random visitors from the perspective of an old woman living in seclusion. Although the story is not entirely devoid of a moral message, it is rather concerned with the ephemeral nature of human life and of the physical world. When compared to *The Life of an Amorous Woman*, Defoe's *Moll Flanders* appears more complex as far as its thematic structure is concerned. Unlike Saikaku's heroine, Moll is not

---

[20] Parts of this monograph were developed on the basis of my M.A. theses "How to Reveal and Conceal: Mode of Confession in Ihara Saikaku's *The Life of an Amorous Woman* and Daniel Defoe's *Moll Flanders*" written under the supervision of Prof. dr hab. Teresa Bela in 2007.

merely obsessed with erotic desire. She is, as Sutherland (1971) observes, "certainly susceptible to attractive men, but she never strikes one as being oversexed, and indeed goes out of her way several times to tell us so" (170). In fact, it is not so much the eroticism but rather the money and independence that thematically prevail in Defoe's work.[21]

The complexity of themes in *Moll Flanders* is reflected in the full title of the book:

> The Fortunes and Misfortunes of the Famous Moll Flanders, Etc. Who was born in Newgate, and during a life of continu'd Variety for Threescore Years, besides her Childhood, was Twelve Year a *Whore*, five times a *Wife* (whereof once to her own brother), Twelve Year a *Thief*, Eight Year a Transported *Felon* in *Virginia*, at last grew *Rich*, liv'd *Honest* and died a *Penitent*. Written from her own Memorandums (MF iii).

The title openly announces three themes important in interpreting the story of Moll's life. Piper (1969) realises that there is also a hierarchy of themes in *Moll Flanders*, indicating "two major topics and a minor one: sexual adventures, adventures in theft and Virginia adventures" (495). Moll in her account swiftly moves from one topic to another. Although in general the themes appear in chronological order, the adventures in Virginia suggest a "cyclical nature of the plot" as they are significantly repetitive (Watt 1967: 110).

More importantly, Defoe seems to be far more interested in the moral aspect of the story his heroine narrates. As Dobrée (1959) realises, "it would not be unfair to say that Defoe's two driving interests were: trade and morals" (56). As a consequence, Moll frequently reflects upon the nature of her deeds, evaluating them in relation to God and natural law, as well as in the context of the prevailing social conventions. The moral goal of Moll's confession is also emphasised in the popular readings of the novel:

---

[21] According to Hühn (2001), "Moll evaluates everything in terms of money… So neither in her marriage schemes nor in her criminal activities is she primarily guided by sensual desire, passion or vice but by money" (337). Kibbie focuses on the relationship between the desire for erotic pleasure and the desire for money intermingled in *Moll Flanders*: "When Moll Flanders' first lover, the elder son of her employers gives her presents of gold, he initiates an association between money and sexual desire that continues throughout her narrative" (Kibbie 1995: 1026). Birdsall also emphasises the importance of money in *Moll Flanders*: "Money is not for Moll an end in itself but a means to the end of ease and comfort in the most elemental sense – a means of achieving a feeling of 'athomeness' in the world and of freedom from fear. She is an accumulator because money is power and lack of it is weakness and vulnerability" (Birdsall 1985: 80).

The elderly Moll Flanders who narrates the story is a woman who is determined to tell her story so it can serve as a deterrent to anyone who might contemplate a life of crime, as an assurance to the sinner that no life is too despicable to be salvaged through repentance (Magill 2009: 674).

Although the thematic structure and focus of the two works differs, there are, nonetheless, noteworthy correspondences between the narrative techniques employed by Saikaku and Defoe. Both writers chose their narrators carefully: women who speak about their lives and their innermost secrets from a perspective of time and space. These apparent similarities in the construction of the narrative voices in *The Life of an Amorous Woman* and *Moll Flanders* encourage a comparative reading of the two texts, which also brings to light the tradition of confessional writings in Japan and England, as well as evokes the implications of the term "confession."

Chapter II. The Strategy of Confession

II.1. The Ambiguity of "Confession"

The term "confession" is at least as ambiguous as the terms "novel" and *shōsetsu* are. John Anthony Cuddon (1992) defines it as a "rather vague category," into which he places "works which are a very personal and subjective account of experiences, beliefs, feelings, ideas, and states of mind, body and soul" (194). In Western tradition it was originally used to denote the declaration of either love or faith. As a consequence, the term is closely associated with both poetry, especially with the romantic or chivalric poetic tradition, and religion (mainly with Christianity). Moreover, the origins of confession are frequently traced back to the oral rather than the written form, as confession was initially connected with the Christian tradition of revealing one's sins and asking for forgiveness (the auricular confession).

In the face of these common implications of the word "confession," any attempts to present Defoe's *Moll Flanders* and Saikaku's *The Life of an Amorous Woman* as examples of confession in prose, or a "fictional confession," may be regarded as adventurous. It may be argued that they both belong to what Cuddon (1992) terms as a "confessional novel," being "a rather misleading and flexible term which suggests an 'autobiographical' type of fiction, written in the first person, and which, on the face of it, is a self-revelation" (194). The expression "on the face of it" introduces space for "confessions" in which the author assumes the role of a character he creates. However, the question what constitutes confession as a genre or a manner of expression in prose has to be addressed. The goals of this chapter are to suggest the possibility of formal traits that might be considered typical of confession and to trace the development of the confessional voice in both Japanese and English literature.

Confession is frequently viewed and analysed in a broader context of autobiographical writing. *The Bloomsbury Guide to English Literature* distinguishes among "three historical segments" of autobiography: the spiritual confession, the memoir and the autobiographical novel (383). According to this distinction, the autobiographical novel is traced back to the "mock-autobiographies of the Elizabethan novel" (384). Contrarily, the spiritual autobiography is characterised by a "detailed account of emotional life" as the focus of the speaker (383). The depiction of one's authentic life and historical events is limited and subordinate to the speaker's private history.

It is possible to say, in a narrow sense, that an autobiography is a story of an individual presented in his or her own voice. As Mandel (1968) claims, "autobiography is a retrospective account of a man's whole life (or a significant part of a life) written as avowed truth and for a specific purpose by a man who lived the life" (217). In a broader sense, however, "autobiography" may indicate "any text in which the author *seems* to express his life or his feelings, whatever the form of the text, whatever the contract proposed by the author" (Lejeune 1989: 123). Therefore, it is not the first-person narration or any other formal stylistic device that constitutes an autobiography but the truthfulness and reliability of the message conveyed by the speaker.

The problem of authenticity is reflected in Philippe Lejeune's concept of the "autobiographical pact" or "autobiographical contract," in which the phenomenon of autobiography is based on the reader's willingness to accept the contract which confirms the identity of the author, reader and narrator. Once the contract is agreed upon, the reader consents to the "authenticity" of the text proposed by the author and starts to identify the narrator and the protagonist with the name on the cover of the book (Lejeune 1975: 13–46).

It seems that according to Lejeune there is hardly anything within the text that would enable the reader to differentiate between the autobiography and the autobiographical novel.[22] The contract the author proposes is the same: an appeal to the readers to accept the sameness of the narrator, the author and the protagonist. This claim is also important in the analysis of how confession may function in works of fiction. Both Saikaku and later Defoe created

---

[22] This notion is controversial as many critics are more eager to accept Barett John Mandel's claim that "the autobiographer (…) may never falsify his facts for a fictional purpose without giving up his claim to the name of autobiographer" (Mandel 1968: 220).

worlds which are experienced and commented upon by two fictitious characters. Nonetheless, the readers are asked to believe in the truthfulness of the narratives and in the honesty of the narrators identified with the protagonists.

II.2. Definition

A concise but explicit definition of confession is included in *The Literary Encyclopaedia*:

> [A] form of autobiography, in which the true or manipulated account of the author's life serves some sort of didactic purpose. In this sense, confessions constitute a literary *genre* which took its start in the *CONFESSIONS OF ST. AUGUSTINE*. They reached the height of their development in the era of romanticism when they began to show symptoms of narcissistic decadence (*The Reader's Encyclopedia: An Encyclopedia of World Literature and the Arts* 235).[23]

This definition is very comprehensive and it gives the post-Enlightenment understanding of the term, which embraces both the real-life and the fictional dimensions of the confession. It indicates its purpose and emphasises its important status in the history of literary genres.

In his study of the art of storytelling, Richard Kearney (2001), theoretician and historian of literature, enumerates various genres, such as "myth, epic, sacred history, legend, saga, folktale, romance, allegory, confession, chronicle, satire, [and] novel" (5). In his classification, confession is granted the status of a genre. Nonetheless, it is most difficult to name a number of objective criteria that would distinguish the confession from other forms of autobiographical writing.

---

[23] *Dictionary of World Literature* defines the confession as a type of autobiography *(q.v.)*, "sometimes honestly intended, sometimes (Rousseau, *Confessions*, pub. posth. 1781–1788) painting the portrait one would like posterity to hold."It is [c]ommon as a title from St. Augustine (345–430); in a flood among the romantics after Rousseau (De Quincey, *Confessions of an Eng. OpiumEater*, 1821; A. de Musset, *Confessions d'un enfant du siècle*, 1836; Chateaubriand , *Memoires d'outre-tombe*, 1811–36, pub. posth. 1849–1850); on to the fiction of the 'true confessions' pulp magazines of today." It distinguishes between "(1) reminiscences: what a man might tell a roomful; their value depends upon the interest of the events he has shared and persons known; (2) autobiography: what he might tell his friends; its value hinges on his character in relation to persons he has known and things done; (3) confessions: what he'd not tell even his friends; its value springs from the intensity of his inner life" (119).

II.3. Disclosure and Its Moral Significance

What is regarded as a common characteristic of the confession is its tendency to reveal the past of an individual to an audience. The noticeable inclination of the speaker/writer to disclose a message which has previously been hidden or kept private enables Lejeune (1989) to call the confession "the centre of the autobiographical domain" (125). Another quality that may be distinctive for the confession is its moral dimension. As quoted above, the confession is believed to "serve some sort of didactic purpose." This didactic or moral goal is strongly related to the idea of the alleged honesty of the speaker/writer and the truthfulness of the message.

As a consequence, Coetzee, rather than focusing on genre, focuses on the "mode" of autobiographical writing that he calls "confession." He claims that the confession is "distinct from the *memoir* or the *apology*" not so much because of generic differences but rather due to the dissimilarity in the tone of the speaker/writer, whose "underlying motive" is to "tell an essential truth about the self" (Coetzee 1985: 194). The message should not only be sincere and reliable but it should also reveal the essence, the fundamental quality of the speaker's inner life.

Francis Hart is even more specific in distinguishing between the modern interpretations of "confession," "apology" and "memoir":

> "Confession" is personal history that seeks to communicate or express the essential nature, the truth, of the self. "Apology" is personal history that seeks to demonstrate or realise the integrity of the self. "Memoir" is personal history that seeks to articulate or repossess the historicity of the self (Hart 1970: 421).

Hart's distinction is based on the different aspects of self that are revealed in three different modes of writing. The confession, just like the apology and the memoir, is a form of disclosure: it reveals the privacy of the self to the public. However, it focuses on the truthfulness of the account, as it should uncover the genuine reality of the individual's life.

If the didactic quality of the confession refers, on the one hand, to a moral attempt made by the writer to disclose his inner self, it also refers to the moral impact the confession may have on the readers. For example, Horovitz focuses on the social role of the confession, which serves to set "an exemplar of moral behaviour to be emulated, or the reverse, an exemplar of immoral behaviour and hence of pitfalls to avoid in one's own life" (Horovitz 1977: 173).

The mode of confession implies that the content of the story, which is important for the writers who reveal their innermost experiences, may be used to influence the reader's moral conduct. Confession serves to reveal the writer's self to the public, and may be said to mediate between the world of the writer and the world of the reader. As a consequence, it is frequently shaped by the readers and their expectations. Moreover, it is often craftily devised to influence the readers. As Mandel notices, the "conception of his [Defoe's] audience is obviously related to his guiding purpose in important ways" (221). In this context it is not surprising that the importance of the readers at whom the confession is targeted is so often emphasised.

Both the self-revelation and the appeal to the public should be regarded as two equally important purposes of the confession. Since it is written to achieve a specific goal "which helps to shape the work and without which there would be no work," the confession may be rightfully referred to as "a literary art in the Aristotelian sense" (Mandel 1968: 217). Therefore, it should be remembered that the confession may influence the readers but that the readers also have, rather paradoxically, an impact on the confession.

As a consequence, the confessional character of Defoe's *Moll Flanders* and Saikaku's *Life of an Amorous Woman* distinguishes the two works from fabliaux, novellas or romances, which are often "content with the story for the story's sake, independent of the conditions of actual life" (Chandler 1907, 1: 286). It is because both Moll and The Amorous Woman reveal their private lives and simultaneously appeal to the audience by proving that their accounts are deeply rooted in what they also may easily relate to.

II.4. Confession and Realism

The confession constitutes a specific link between the inner and the outer realities and thus involves the questions of imitation and realistic representation. In fact, there seems to be a close relationship between the confession and realism. First of all, the message conveyed by the speaker or writer relies on introspection and observation rather than on fancy or imagination. It is therefore not unexpected that the critics emphasise Defoe's use of the "observational method" and his impressive "realistic temperament" (Chandler 1907, 2: 286). As a genre of observation, the confession as written by Defoe should be considered a true manifestation of the eighteenth-century sensibility.

44

Ihara Saikaku is also highly appreciated for his realistic descriptive technique. Of course, it should be remembered that – as Susumu Hiroshima (1993) aptly notices – it is only by the end of the nineteenth century that the Japanese critics introduced the term "realism" into their literary discourse (153–154). It is important to acknowledge that Saikaku's realism, especially his realistic depiction of man's sexual desire, was praised mostly by writers and critics fascinated by naturalism.[24] Later, a number of critics began to appreciate his use of detail and enumeration. Yamashita (1966), for example, claims that "in the history of Japanese literature, Saikaku was renowned for his writings which depict in greatest detail the reality of Edo times" (25). Hibbett (1954) also emphasises Saikaku's realistic portrayal of his times: "the atmosphere of that urban society: its iconoclasm, its fervid emotional tone, its spontaneous gaiety and exuberance, restrained chiefly by aesthetic refinement and an exacting code of manners" (411). Berry (2006) notes that "[a]s vigorously as any author of a gazetteer or urban directory, Saikaku, too, counts and calculates, lists and labels. He delights in things of wonder, and in things made wonderful by their names and variety and plenitude" (31). Lane (1959) speaks of the "skillful use of 'exterior correctness'" in Boccaccio's and Saikaku's literature which he relates to the possible interest in painting the two writers showed (98). Undoubtedly, Saikaku's brilliant observations enabled him to depict (often through imitation) the reality of the seventeenth-century Japanese towns and their inhabitants.

However, the term "realism" needs to be applied to Ihara Saikaku's literary achievements with proper care. As already mentioned, it was first used by the writers of the Meiji era, who emphasised Saikaku's interest in social matters. Shimamura Hōgetsu, Tayama Katai, and Masamune Hakuchō were among those who rediscovered the author of *The Life of an Amorous Woman* as a realist (Shimamura 1975: 1–38). Nonetheless, as Hibbett (1954) indicates, the "genroku realism" might be considered "a particular set of literary techniques," with "no dislike of fancy or inconsistency" and "no predilection for an objective plain style" or "full-blown rational description" (417–418). It may be argued that Saikaku's narratives aimed at satirical rather than realistic depiction and this satire "may in retrospect have the appearance of realism" as it is rooted in the social and economic circumstances of its time (Johnson 2001: 337).

---

[24] Among the writers who were fascinated by Saikaku's realistic techniques were Shimamura Hōgetsu, Tayama Katai, and Masamune Hakuchō (Shimizu 1965: 49–54; Teruoka 1949: 332–338).

II.5. Religious Origins

Since the confession in Europe is originally related to the disclosure of one's trespasses, most critics interpret it in reference to religious practices. Even Gower's *Confessio Amantis*, although referring to a lover's confession, can be put in the same category, as it focuses on the trespasses against "courtly love," or the "religion of love." As the poet emphasises: "That Love is falle into discorde…That Love is fro the world departed" (Gower 1889: 35). Therefore, it seems that the tendency to analyse one's true self in prose should also be traced back to what Lehmann calls the "innate tendencies toward self-examination and the insistence on the obligation of regarding God as the ultimate Judge and Redeemer of the individual" (Lehmann 1953: 42). Lehmann's comment reflects the Protestant idea that the relationship between men and God is most private and confidential, and it does not require or allow any intermediary.

Coetzee, in his brilliant analysis of the confession, also overtly refers to the religious provenance of the phenomenon. He claims: "Confession is one element in a sequence of transgression, confession, penitence and absolution. Absolution means the end of the episode, the closing of the chapter, liberation from the oppression of memory" (Coetzee 1985: 194). This, however, does not define confession in terms of the Protestant direct relation between God and the individual. For Coetzee, the confession is closer to the Catholic interpretation, as it forms a stage in the process of receiving absolution.

If in Europe the confession is interpreted in the context of Christianity, in Japan it may be related to the Buddhist concept of *sange* or *zange* (literally: penitence or penance).[25] Margaret Childs distinguishes between *sange* meaning "meditative or devotional practice" in Buddhism and its "literary transformation" taking a form of *zange monogatari* or "revelatory tales."[26] She explains the significance of the *sange* practice:

---

[25] Robert Aitken explains the differences between *sange* and European notions of confession and that of sin in general. He also refers to the prominent work by Quentin Donaghue and Linda Shapiro, who analyse the Catholic confession (*Bless Me Father for I have Sinned: Catholics Speak out about Confession*. New York: Donald I. Fine, 1984) (Aitken 2002: 70).

[26] Childs further explains she uses the word "revelation" – "in its first and general meaning in English: 'the act of revealing what was unknown before" and not in the Judeo-Christian theological sense of the act of God revealing divine truth to man." She insists that "there is

> Realizing that past emotional attachments hinder enlightenment, we renounce them in order to devote ourselves exclusively to the cultivation of an understanding of religious truths, knowledge of which emancipates us from pain and suffering. Sange was the practice of meditatively reviewing those attachments in order to deepen the previously experienced realization of transience (Childs 1987: 53).

Sange served to purify the "six organs of sensation" (de Visser 1935: 251). The Buddhist penitence does not stem, however, from the realization of the Original Sin or of any particular trespasses. It is rather the effect of the recognition of the original, essential purity of the world which is marred by the "evil karma" as quoted in the ritual confession popular among Sōtō and Rinzai Buddhists:[27]

> All the evil karma, ever created by me since of old,
> On account of my beginningless greed, hatred and ignorance,
> Born of my conduct, speech and thought,
> I now confess openly and fully (Suzuki 1935: 47).

There are a few similarities between the *sange* quoted above and the Catholic act of confession. The expression "conduct, speech and thought" parallels the Catholic "thought, word and deed." What brings Buddhism closer to Protestantism is the belief that there is no mediation between the human being and Buddha: "ultimately one confesses, repents and is forgiven in the non-dual purity of the self and Buddha" (Kim 1987: 205).[28] Moreover, it is not uncommon for the Buddhist confession to be endowed with not only private but also social importance. Suzuki (1935) notices that "public confession and repentance are classically a part of conflict resolution in the Buddhist community" (71). In this respect, on the surface at least, Buddhist practices are not entirely dissimilar from Christian ones.

Nonetheless, it cannot be overlooked that the nature of God as professed by Christianity and that of Buddha differ conspicuously, as does the notion of man. Accordingly, the idea of confession is also different. While the Christian

---

both a public and a private sense," in which she uses the phrase: "the act of revealing what was unknown before." She also adds that "in the public sense revelatory tales depict a 'revealing to others' Zange is often used in this simple sense of 'making public,' as the word 'confession' is sometimes used in English" (Childs 1987: 54).

[27] Buddhism is not a unified system of dogmas but that it has many schools and sects which differ conspicuously in their preaching.

[28] Yukio Matsudo (2000) notices interesting similarities between the modern Buddhist rituals and Protestant practices (59–69).

confession refers to the sins committed throughout one's lifetime, the Buddhist *sange* embraces "the evil karma ever created" and thus it demonstrates how the repentance is formed in opposition to the original state of purity.

The impact of Christianity on the development of the confessional voice in European prose is not to be overlooked. Similarly, the role of Buddhist practices cannot be ignored. However, it seems that rather than being determined by any particular religion, the confession reflects the natural and cross-cultural quality of human beings who tend to disclose their private, inner lives to others. Moreover, although the religious contexts are important, the confessional narratives both in England and in Japan developed far beyond them. As Childs points out, they move from repentance to revelation. She explains the revelatory character of Japanese *zange monogatari*:

> Revelatory tales in which characters make a kind of statement of faith by describing the sorrows that result from ignorance and illusion, are not the flowering of a long, latent, secular tradition, as Japanese scholars to date have suggested. Instead, they are a significantly new phenomenon in Japanese literature. As the self-consciously public description of a profound self revelation, revelatory tales are the secular literary manifestation of the concept of *sange* as found in Buddhist scripture and appear for the first time during the medieval period. Thus, a religious ritual inspired the creation of a new literary genre (63).

The tradition of Buddhist confession contributed to the rise of *zange monogatari*, a new literary genre in Japan. Gradually, confession was transformed into revelation and the writers' urge to reveal inspired the development of the modern novel.

II.6. Tradition of Confession in Japan

Most of the implications that the term "confession" has in the West are irrelevant to Japan. It would have been unwise to speak about Christian confession in pre-modern Japan. Although Christianity was not wholly absent from the Japanese isles in the times of Saikaku, it was officially prohibited and its influence was first restricted only to certain areas in Kyushu and gradually stifled.[29] Moreover, the literature of confession had already been

---

[29] Saint Francis Xavier started his mission in Kagoshima, Japan in 1549. Between 1609 and 1614 Christianity was gradually banned in Japan.

48

flourishing in Japan long before the first missionaries came bringing with them the achievements of Christian thought and rite.

The *zange monogatari* (or *zange mono*) mentioned before were one area of influence. The narrative structure of those "tales of revelation" was intricate: it "takes the form of two or more monks or nuns telling each other in turn how they came to their religious awakenings" (Childs 1987: 54). The tales had existed long before the name "zange monogatari" appeared. Its use is recorded in the early seventeenth century.

In Japan all autobiographical genres or modes of expression were referred to by one name, *nikki*, which embraced the meanings of diaries, memoirs, confessions and even autobiographical novels.[30] As the term *nikki* or "daily notes" suggests, the structure of the text is often chronological as the narration traces the events of subsequent days, but otherwise it is difficult to find any consistently common traits of the genre (Keene 1999b: 1). *Nikki* are sometimes divided into three subcategories: official diaries documenting the events of the imperial court, private diaries written by aristocrats, and notes taken during various contests of poetry (Cranston 1969: 90). The distinction between the official and the private diaries is frequently substantiated by the use of two different writing systems depending on the purpose of the text: classical Chinese (*kanbun*) for the former, and Japanese *wabun* style with *kana* syllabary for the latter (Keene 1995: 29). However, the distinction between the private and the public for official purposes is often far from ambiguous (Mostow 2004: 1).

The fact that the term *nikki* was used to denote such a variety of genres and modes of writing may indicate that the distinction between fiction and autobiography or between imagination and reality was of minor importance for writers and readers in Japan. As Earl Miner (1968) notices, the "narrow margin between truth and fiction is presumed to be much narrower, one can see, in Japanese literature" (41). The term also embraced fiction written in a manner of a diary until a new term, *nikki bungaku* or "literary diaries," was introduced. The new term appeared only at the beginning of the twentieth century, even though the first examples of *nikki bungaku* date back to the ninth century.

---

[30] Donald Keene gives a detailed account of the history of *nikki*-writing in Japan in his two volumes: *Travellers of a Hundred Ages: The Japanese As Revealed Through 1,000 Years of Diaries* (1999) and *Modern Japanese Diaries: The Japanese at Home and Abroad As Revealed Through Their Diaries* (1995).

The comprehensive quality of the term may also be related to the predominant attitude towards private fiction in pre-modern and early-modern Japan, where it was not considered significant enough to be examined in greater detail or in a systematic manner. In opposition to poetry, which was extensively studied and analysed, non-official or even vernacular prose was widely neglected by critics and scholars.

Private writing in prose was juxtaposed with poetry, which was regarded as something superior to prose, the embodiment of truth (*makoto*) or pure beauty. As a consequence poetry was the ideal subject matter for scholars. It could be written and performed only by well-educated people (mostly men) since it required a vast knowledge of Chinese literature and was written either in Chinese or by means of *man'yōgana* (a specific writing system where Chinese characters are used to render Japanese phonemes). It was most honourable to compose poetry, and rather disreputable to indulge in writing private diaries. Therefore, a well-educated notable in pre-modern Japan would boast about his poems as much as he would refrain from admitting to having written a private account in prose. In this context, the frequent use of poetry in private or literary diaries may also be regarded as an attempt to enhance their artistic value (Miner 1968: 44).

The literature of *nikki* was considered to be the domain of women writers, who became more numerous in the Heian Period (named for the imperial capital which was the centre of political and aesthetic influence through the ninth to eleventh century). The life in Heian-kyō (contemporary Kyoto), in the court of the emperor, generously provided the ladies-in-waiting and the wives of the aristocrats with both inspiration and free time. As a consequence, the women started writing down their impressions, remarks and dreams in a form of *nikki*. Since they were not that well acquainted with the Chinese language, they started using a new writing system – a phonetic syllabary (*kana*), later known as the "woman's hand" (*onnade*). The artistic value of the diaries written in the "woman's hand" is unquestionable. Most of the fine examples of the confessional prose from Heian: *Izumi Shikibu Nikki* (*The Diary of Izumi Shikibu*, 1002–1003), *Murasaki Shikibu Nikki* (*The Diary of Murasaki Shikibu*, 1008–1010), and *Sarashina Nikki* (*Sarashina Diary*, 1059–1062), are still widely read in modern times.

One of the most prominent confessions of the Heian period was the *Kagerō Nikki* (*The Gossamer Diary*) written by a lady known as *Michitsuna no haha* (the Mother of Michitsuna) who lived in the tenth century (c. 935–995).

In her account, the Mother of Michitsuna depicted the life she led as the wife of Kaneie, a distinguished aristocrat of the Fujiwara family. Her diaries are recognized by modern critics as the "prototype of the journalistic style that would be typical of women writers" (Ruch 1994: 405).

To what extent *nikki* was meant as a genre for women may be proved by the fact that the famous poet Ki no Tsurayuki (879–945) decided to hide his true identity in order to write a poetic diary. His *Tosa Nikki* (*Tosa Diary*) starts with an introduction in which the author insists on his being a woman. He also uses the phonetic syllabary instead of the Chinese signs, which he had used before, e.g. in his treatise on poetry opening *Kokinwakashū*, a famous anthology of Japanese poetry.

There is a noticeable parallel between *Tosa Nikki* and both Saikaku's and Defoe's works – the male authors are writing from a woman's point of view and adopting a style they consider suitable for the purpose. However, while Tsurayuki needed the female alias in order to express himself freely in a genre that was not appreciated at the time, Saikaku and Defoe deliberately choose women's voices to speak about women's experience from their own perspectives. In the case of Saikaku, the treatment of both *nikki* literature and *sange/zange* tradition is noticeably satirical leading to what is known as *irozange* or "love confession" imbued with eroticism (Eubanks 2011: 217).

II.7. Tradition of Confession in England

The confessional mode of writing in England has been greatly influenced by St. Augustine of Hippo, who, in his *Confessions* (397–398), displayed the inward reality of the self and presented his spiritual journey to God. The work was also to set an example of man's conversion and devotion. Echoes of St. Augustine can be heard in the work of St. Patrick written a century later. Bruce Hindmarsh notices that St. Patrick's *Confession* was even more audience-oriented, since the missionary wanted to defend himself against accusations concerning his mission in Ireland. Hindmarsh also perceives certain similarities between St. Patrick's *Confession* and the royal conversion narratives of Clovis of the Franks in the fifth century, Ethelbert of Kent in the sixth century, and Edwin of Northumbria in the seventh century (Hindmarsh 2005: 22).

Although there are a few "records of the inner life" in the Middle Ages, such as *The Book of Margery Kempe* (15th century), in the seventeenth century the confession began to flourish (*The Bloomsbury Guide to English Literature* 383). An important stage in the development of the confession in England was the publication of Richard Kilby's *The Burthen of a Loaden Conscience* (1608), which is regarded as an example of the Puritan conversion narrative. It is, however, far from being a pure confession. As Hindmarsh notices, "it is something of a hybrid or transitional genre: part self-examination and confession, part biblical exposition, part sermonic exhortation, and part factual narrative" (Hindmarsh 2005: 39). A similar combination of modes and styles is characteristic of both Saikaku and Defoe.

Most of all, the conversion narratives were recognised for their moralistic purpose. They conveyed the Puritan message of faith, which belonged to the private world of the believers, to the public. Even closer to the original meaning of the term "confession" were John Bunyan's statements of faith as expressed in *A Confession of My Faith, And a Reason of my Practice* (1672).[31] This work is also a vivid manifestation of Bunyan's theological beliefs.

The conversion narratives were confessions made in public. There was, however, also a more private realisation of Puritan "imperatives of careful bookkeeping and assiduous self-reckoning" which took a form of a diary or journal (Sherman 2005: 651). There was even a guidebook to diary-keeping (*The Journal or Diary of a Thankful Christian*) written by John Beadle and published in 1656, which resonates with the mode and tone of Defoe's *Robinson Crusoe*. Beadles words "what better means can be used for the advancement of faith in the growth and strength of it, then a rich treasure of experience; every experiment of Gods favour to us, being a good prop for our faith for the future" (quoted in Sherman 2005: 652) best summarise the development of Defoe's famous protagonist.

If the Puritan conversion narrative affected the mode of writing in *Moll Flanders*, the literary tradition of roguery highly influenced its subject-matter. Stories of villains, colourful enough to attract readers and parabolic enough to perform a didactic function, became increasingly popular in the early sixteenth century. As Frank Wadleigh Chandler (1907) realises, "works as various as 'Eulenspiegel,' the 'Fourberies de Scapin,' the ballades of Villon, the 'Beggar's Opera,' a felon's confession, and a sociological study of criminals

---

[31] It is difficult to agree with Needleman and Otis (1938) who claim that a statement of Bunyan's theology "is essentially an explanation of his prejudices'" (316).

may fall within the genre" (1: 1). Moreover, not only the literary tradition but also Defoe's acquaintances, among others John Applebee, a printer of "criminals' confessions and biographies" (Chandler 1907, 2: 287), might have had an impact on the thematic composition of his novel.

Daniel Defoe, well-known for his *Colonel Jack, Moll Flanders* and *Roxana*, had in fact many predecessors writing about the lives of rakes and rascals.[32] In the mid-sixteenth century Thomas Harman's *Caveat of Common Cursitors* (1566), and John Awdeley's *Fraternity of Vagabonds* (1561) gave account of the adventures of sharp-witted criminals. Later, Robert Greene (1558–1592), the author of *Groats-Worth of Wit* (1592), Thomas Nashe (1567–1601), the author of *The Unfortunate Traveller* (1594), and Samuel Rowlands (c. 1573–1630), also focused on outlaws playing various roles in their stories. Both Greene and Nashe used "spoken dialectic" and improvisation, techniques present in most of Defoe's novels.

II.8. Syncretism of Genres

Before analysing the confessional voices in the two works, it necessary to clarify that, although *The Life of an Amorous Woman* and *Moll Flanders* are compared here as two works using the mode of confession, they are both very complex and unequivocal as far as genre is concerned.[33]

In fact, in most books on Japanese literature Saikaku's *The Life of an Amorous Woman* is given the status of a *monogatari* (story), *ukiyozōshi* (story of the "floating world") or *kōshoku mono*, rather than the one of a confession. The first term emphasises the narrative strategy and the fictional character of Saikaku's work. The second and the third focus on its subject-matter or

---

[32] Chandler (1907) explains the literary phenomenon of the "anatomy of roguery": "The anatomy of roguery may be defined as an essay descriptive of the grades, cheats, or manners of professional criminals. It embraces such works as the beggar–books of Awdeley and Harman; the conny-catching pamphlets of Greene, Dekker, and Rowlands; the prison tracts of Hutton, Fennor, and Mynshul; the later discoveries of criminal mysteries by the repentant; canting lexicons and scoundrel verse; and modern sociological studies of crime" (1: 87).

[33] Bell (1958) speaks about the syncretism of genres in *Moll Flanders*: *Moll Flanders* "might even be seen as a compilation or permutation of the criminal biography, the confessional, and the pamphlet on social policy, with occasional intervention of pornography, scandal, sheet anecdote, and transportation tale. The effect of these various references is that reading is not strictly supervised by any one *genre*, and the tale's idiosyncrasies become foregrounded" (158).

the prevailing theme. Similarly, Defoe's *Moll Flanders* is considered either a novel or a biography or – as Howard Hibbett calls it – "erotic picaresque" (Hibbett 1959: 36) far more frequently than a confession. Undoubtedly the eighteenth century was marked by the development of biography. In 1791, some decades after *Moll Flanders*, James Boswell published life *Life of Samuel Johnson*, a biography including Johnson's quotations which Boswell did not hesitate to alter to suit his vision, which remains one of the most appreciated biographies written in English. Among the picaresque predecessors of *Moll Flanders* was *La Pícara Justina* (published in Spanish in 1605), which may also be considered an example of criminal biography, developed and refined by Defoe (Richetti 2005: 235).

There are numerous genres which Saikaku and Defoe might have turned to for inspiration. Defoe is said to have been strongly influenced by "seventeenth-century books of travel, memoirs, history, biographies, autobiographies, not forgetting the spiritual biographies and autobiographies of Nonconformist circles, [and] day-to-day journalism" (Wilson 1960: 23). One may argue, however, that all of these genres are related to the confessional mode of his novels. However, in the background of *Moll Flanders* there is not only the tradition of confession but also of so-called non-heroic genres such as "fabliaux, farces and popular tales" (Rodrigues-Luis 1979: 33). It is possible to argue, as Richetti (1999) does, that "[l]iterature and literary tradition, even the diluted picaresque and spiritual autobiography out of which Defoe fashions his narratives, are institutions that work to defuse the potentially disturbing individuality of his narrators" (55). The situation is not too dissimilar in Saikaku's writings, which were also influenced by books of travels, lives of famous actors and courtesans, folktales, popular songs and *kabuki* or *bunraku* plays.

Many critics perceive the picaresque novel as the main source of Defoe's inspiration. Sutherland focuses on the picaresque manner of depicting thievery in *Moll Flanders* (Sutherland 1971: 192). Similarly, Dazinger speaks about "the rogue biography in *Moll Flanders* and *Jonathan Wild*" and its "relation to the picaresque tradition" (Danziger 1962: 648). Robert Alter focuses on Moll's being both candid and immoral, which he considers a crucial characteristic of a picaro.[34] Finally, Rodreigues-Luis analyses the realistic

---

[34] "Since he has no set place in society and is not committed to the established order, he is free from the tribute of lip service to conventional morality which most people feel is expected

54

representation of the world and motivation in *Moll Flanders* comparing it to the depiction of other famous picaros. He notices:

> The picaro's hope of achieving his life's goal must be based on a degree of probability ranging from the nearly impossible (in the prologue of *Lazarillo de Tormes* the narrator claims that his achievement equals that of the greatest noblemen) to actual success (in *Moll Flanders*, 1722) (Rodrigues-Luis 1979: 39).

A comparative approach to Defoe's work proves that there are many similarities between Moll and Spanish picaros. It appears that these correspondences in the depiction of the protagonists' adventures may not be coincidental, which encouraged Paulson (1967) to examine to what extent English novels were influenced by Spanish picaresque: he compares *Don Thomaso, or the Juvenile Rambles of Thomas Dangerfield* (1680) to *Lazarillo de Tormes* and *Guzman de Alfarache* (41). He claims that whereas Spanish (mostly Catholic) writers focused on society, and the progress of their protagonist was "not moral at all but prudential," English (mostly Protestant) writers focussed on the individual and his life towards conversion (43). Other critics also emphasise that at the beginning of the eighteenth century, shortly before Defoe started writing the adventures of Moll Flanders, many of the famous Spanish picaresque novels, such as *Garduña de Sevilla, La Picara Justina, Celestina,* and *Estevanillo Gonzalez*, had been translated into English.[35]

To what extent Moll Flanders follows the pattern of a traditional picaro is, nonetheless, debatable. Guillen indicates that a typical *picaro* should be a young orphan who is "obliged to fend for himself ... in an environment for which he is not prepared" (79) and progresses "horizontally through space and vertically through society" (83).

---

from them. He can call a thief a thief and a whore a whore, even when he is the thief and his wife is a whore" (Alter 1964: 38).

[35] Chandler (1907) claims: "Fresh English renderings of the Spanish novels were not lacking. The *Garduña* was compressed from Davies's earlier version, and became *The Life of Donna Rosina* (c. 1700). Its inserted *novelas* were separately issued as *Three Ingenious Spanish Novels* (1712), and L'Estrange and Ozell made a fresh translation of the whole (1717, 1727). Cervantes *Novelas* was Englished in part by Ozell (1709), and was redone by other hands in 1928 and 1729. Captain John Stevens issued *The Comical Works of Quevedo* (1707, 1709, 1742), and upon this was based the version of Pedro Pineda (1743). Stevens, too, in *The Spanish Libertines* (1707) presented to English readers *La Picara Justina, Celestina,* and *Estevanillo Gonzalez*; and the *Celestina* and *Guzman* in 1708 came once more into English through the French. Even *Lazarillo*, unwearied by its sixteenth and seventeenth century vogue, reappeared in 1708 and 1726, while Quevedo's *Visions* was read in versions of 1702, 1708, and 1715" (2: 285–286).

From what we know, Moll does not necessarily fulfil all the criteria of a picaresque life. She is, indeed, brought up among strangers but many of them are kind and understanding. Furthermore, she is a half-orphan, and her life is thus marked by the characteristic "absence of conventional social ties" (Watt 1988: 15).[36] However, her mother does reappear in her life and even plays an important role in the development of the story. Ian Watt notices that the tone of Moll's adventures is also far more solemn than that of typical picaresque novels:

> Some of Moll Flanders's actions may be very similar to those of the *picaro*, but the feeling evoked by them is of a much more complete sympathy and identification: author and reader alike cannot but take her and her problems much more seriously (Watt 1957: 94).

According to Watt, it is not so much the events described in *Moll Flanders* but the mood and attitude which enable the readers to identify with the heroine in her misfortunes. Although Moll may be similar to an outcast or a *picaro* in some respects, her life and personal choices resemble the lives and choices of the readers.

As a consequence, a number of critics oppose the idea that *Moll Flanders* should be read as an example of picaresque fiction. Wilson claims that Defoe's work – as opposed to the picaresque novel – "is not vulgar, debased, facetious; it is serious and on the surface at any rate morally earnest" (Wilson 1960: 23). Indeed, the tone of *Moll Flanders* is frequently plain and measured, more typical of the thoughtful journalistic style than of adventure fiction.[37]

To speak of Saikaku's *Amorous Woman* as a picaresque novel is much more debatable, although not entirely impossible. Saikaku's protagonist travels across Japan as she progresses from one episode to another. She visits various places and experiences different styles of life. Although she is not an orphan, the bonds with her parents are far from tight and from an early

---

[36] Watt notices that most of Defoe's heroes are characteristically portrayed as outcasts: "For the most part, Defoe's heroes either have no family, like Moll Flanders, Colonel Jacque and Captain Singleton, or leave it at an early age never to return, like Roxana and Robinson Crusoe. Not too much importance can be attached to this fact, since adventure stories demand the absence of conventional social ties" (Watt 1988: 15).

[37] It would also be interesting to see how themes and motifs explored in *Moll Flanders* were reread and reinterpreted in later eighteenth-century novels. Foster, who investigates the intertextuality and possible influences exerted by *Moll Flanders*, notices, for example, that Defoe's novel resembles *Manon Lescaut*, "a passion drama of a fated, deathless love and of regeneration" (Foster 1949: 52–53).

56

age she has to learn how to survive on her own. Any similarities to the pica-resque novel, however, can be only coincidental, since it is difficult to speak about this literary tradition in seventeenth-century Japan.

The journey of Saikaku's protagonist should rather be viewed in the context of Japanese *tabi nikki* (travel diaries, often referred to as *kikōbun*) written both in prose and poetry with *Tosa Nikki*, *Sarashina Nikki* and Matsuo Bashō's *Nozarashi Kikō* (*The Record of a Weather-Exposed Skeleton*, 1684), published only two years before Saikaku's work. *Kōshoku Ichidai Onna*, which explores the motif of journey and the mechanism of movement for narrative and satirical purposes, may also be said to anticipate later *kokkei-bon* (comic books) popular through the eighteenth and ninteenth centuries, such as *Tōkaidōchū hizakurige* (*By Shank's Mare Along the Tokaidō*, 1802–1822) by Jippensha Ikkū, in which the movement of two main characters is a predominant narrative strategy.

The preliminary reflections on the nature of confession and the indication of the complex narrative construction of both *The Life of an Amorous Woman* and *Moll Flanders* are a prelude to the following two chapters, which focus on the confessional character of the works.

Chapter III. Conventions of Confession

To what extent Ihara Saikaku's *The Life of an Amorous Woman* and Daniel Defoe's *Moll Flanders* comply with the definition of confession is a question that cannot be answered without detailed analysis and interpretation of both texts. This chapter will therefore examine some characteristic features of the confessional mode in the two works, including the reliability of the speakers, the realistic representation, and the didactic purpose or moral message.

III.1. The Speaker Who Reveals

As indicated in the previous chapter, the principal characteristic of all confessional writing is disclosure. It means that the speaker or writer makes a courageous attempt to reveal the hidden story of their life. In this respect, it seems that both the Amorous Woman and Moll Flanders may be rightly considered confessors. They both write about the most secret aspects of their past. The Amorous Woman, who found her shelter in a monk's hut, is already at a decrepit age, "bent double with age – age that had frosted her hair and made her eyes dim as the waning moon" (AW 122). Her old age and the seclusion of her shelter enable her to speak freely and at length about her life. She reveals the story of her first lover, describes in detail her passions and desires, and confesses openly her acts of abortion. Word after word she leads the readers through the chambers of her lovers. With great passion the woman describes both her sexual intercourses and her moments of true devotion. For example, she confesses how she misses one of her lovers:

> As I read them (the letters), I felt that I was truly in the presence of my lover… Having perused each letter several times, I would place it next to my body when I retired alone to bed. I would fall into a slumber and dream that this letter had assumed my very own form and was talking through the night (AW 155).

In this manner, the Amorous Woman discloses her past deeds and her present fancies. She opens her heart before strangers to be able to finally conclude:

> As I am but a single woman, it seemed bootless to hide anything. I have revealed my whole life to you, from the day when the lotus of my heart first opened, until its petals withered (AW 208).

The use of the poetic simile may be regarded as typical of the style of the narrator, a former courtesan. The parallels and analogies in description are used to appeal to the senses (and evoke the experience) of the audience.

Moll Flanders resembles the Amorous Woman in that she is also elderly and apparently detached from her past. She speaks from the position of a married and secured woman who has gone through difficulties but has also managed to survive:

> [W]e are now grown Old: I am come back to *England*, being almost seventy Years of Age, my Husband sixty-eight, having perform'd much more than the limited Terms of my Transportation: And now notwithstanding all the Fatigues, and all the Miseries we have both gone thro', we are both of us in good Heart and Health (MF 342).

Before, however, she reaches the happy ending, she reveals the various misfortunes she has experienced in her long life. She starts with describing herself as "a poor desolate Girl without Friends, without Cloathes, without Help or Helper in the World" (MF 8). Then, she discloses the details of her first love affair, which led her to become, at least symbolically, "a Whore to one Brother, and a Wife to the other" (MF 31). She reveals many of her manipulations and seductions, her acts of thievery and abuse, her satisfactions and fears. The readers learn about her disguises, travels, arrest and deportation. Here is how she describes the prison of Newgate:

> I was carried to *Newgate*; that horrid Place! my very Blood chills at the mention of its Name; the Place, where so many of my Comrades had been lock'd up, and from whence they went to the fatal Tree; the Place where my Mother suffered so deeply, where I was brought into the World, and from whence I expected no Redemption but by an infamous Death: To conclude, the Place that had so long expected me (MF 273).

As opposed to the artistic style of the Amorous Woman, Moll's expressions are usually plain and direct. Some critics refer to her style as "homely."[38] Undoubtedly, the language she uses contributes greatly to the realism of her story.

---

[38] Novak uses this expression in his description of Defoe's style: "Some curiosities in Defoe's grammar have led other critics to comment on his 'homely' style, but here Defoe is

Although the problem of Saikaku's and Defoe's realism will be discussed later in the chapter, I would now like to emphasise the stylistic and lexical differences in the confession made by the Amorous Woman and that of Moll. Defoe does not resort to poetic figures; Moll's description is unembellished and simple. What Sutherland (1971) calls the "plain-spoken, down-to-earth, unpedantic and colloquial style" (74) may be traced back to Defoe's journalistic endeavours.[39] However, in Defoe's works of fiction the journalistic style helps to create the plausibility of the depicted world. If we agree with Preston that "the plain style is really a test of good faith; it is an *exercise* in honesty, for the reader as well as for the writer" (Preston 1970: 19), we may also believe that the plainness of Moll's language is to prove her sincerity. It may be, therefore, argued that Moll's style is well suited to the idea of the confession which itself is "exercise in honesty".[40]

In the case of Saikaku's Amorous Woman the use of style and language is far more figurative. It is not infrequent to hear the woman quoting a classical poem or playing with poetic associations. Again, we may explain it by referring to the techniques Saikaku used in his humorous linked verses (*haikai*). Nonetheless, despite a number of incongruities, it is also true that the style of the Amorous Woman, who was brought up among the emperor's ladies-in-waiting, is used to evoke the atmosphere of the gallant pastimes and of the pleasure quarters.

III.2. Professed Reliability

However captivating and impressive a confession might be, it will not be entirely convincing if the confessor is not reliable and trustworthy. It is not sur-

---

taking advantage either of what would be Moll's ungrammatical manner or simply sacrificing grammar to achieve a sense of grammar and excitement" (Novak 1970: 363).

[39] The introduction to *Captain Singleton* refers to Defoe's *Review* (vii 1710, no. 39) to prove his use of plain style: "[Defoe] himself never failed to remind his readers, particularly of the *Review*, that he had deliberately 'chosen a downright plainness, and to speak home both in fact and style' because it would be 'more generally instructing and clear to the understanding of the people I am speaking to" (*Captain Singleton* xviii).

[40] Sutherland associates the plainness of Defoe's style with honesty: "[Defoe) habitually wrote plain English, called a rogue a rogue, and a whore a whore, and continually reduced moral and religious problems, political issues, and economic policies to the simplest terms. (…) Defoe's black-and-white view of things undoubtedly leads at times to oversimplification" (Sutherland 1971: 132).

prising then that in both *Moll Flanders* and *The Life of an Amorous Woman* the narrators, who speak under fictitious names, are nonetheless presented as authentic people whose words can be trusted. However, the ways in which their credibility is achieved differ slightly in the two works.

Saikaku begins the story of the Amorous Woman with a saying from "the ancients" and a short introductory narrative written from the perspective of a young man. In this manner he introduces the theme of the confession:

> A beautiful woman – so the ancients say – is an axe that cuts off a man's very life. The blossoms scatter, the trees wither away, and when evening comes all are thrown into the hearth and burned. Even so is it with the flower of the human heart; for death is the fate that no one can escape (AW 121).

The woman's account is preceded (and objectified) by the words of wisdom, and then by the man's comments. At the same time, the character of the listener of the woman's confession is also sketched.

Saikaku first gives all the details of the man's journey, placing it specifically in time and space: "It was on the Day of Man (i.e. the seventh day of the First Moon) that I set forth on an errand to Saga in the western purlieus of the capital" (AW 120). Using the man's own words, Saikaku carefully depicts the whereabouts of the hermitage where "an old lady of noble visage" is waiting for the travellers. He notices: "Here stood a sparse hedge of withered clover; a gate, fashioned of bamboo grass, had fallen into ruin, and a dog's track led through the undergrowth" (AW 122).

Although the hermitage is decrepit and ruined, its dweller seems "immune to the ravages of her years" (AW 122). The respectability and nobility of the old lady is emphasized in the introductory paragraph. It appears that the male narrator not only establishes the reliability of the woman but also sparks the reader's interest in her story with an impassioned plea: "Pray tell us afresh of your own rich past" (AW 123). In this manner, Saikaku prepares the grounds for the woman's confession.

Unlike Saikaku, Defoe enables his heroine to speak overtly from the very first paragraph of the novel. However, he also prepares a suitable explanation for her confession, as he provides the book with an instructive and explicit authorial preface. In the beginning of the "Preface" he admits that "[t]he World is so taken up of late with Novels and Romances, that it will be hard for a private History to be taken for Genuine" (MF 1). Nonetheless, he insists on the reliability of Moll Flanders and the authenticity of her story.

He also acknowledges that 'the Stile of the famous Lady we here speak of is a little alter'd' (MF 1), as he himself revised and refined her language to make it 'fit to be read' (MF 1). The insistence on factuality and truthfulness is characteristic also of *Robinson Crusoe.*

Although some modern critics tend to emphasise the male and paternalistic import of the "Preface," it is also possible to argue that it was created to emphasise Defoe's authority as an author and as a self-acknowledged witness to Moll's story.[41] In this manner, the editor's testimony may serve to underpin Moll's confession.

It is worth remembering that in Defoe's times it was not uncommon to justify in the preface the author's claim "to be writing fact rather than fiction" (Rothschild 1990: 26).[42] This practice stemmed from the idea, expressed as early as the 4th century B.C. by Plato and embraced later by the Puritans, that fiction was immoral and, thus, harmful. As Leopold Darmosh aptly comments, "[a] committed Puritan had no use for fiction, despising it as a form of lying and as an inexcusable preoccupation with worldly things" (Darmosh 1988: 90). Above all, writers tended to justify their scenes of criminality by indicating in the preface their realistic provenance and moral significance.[43] It is therefore not surprising to see such a justification preceding the confession of a former thief.

Defoe's comments on the editorial changes and omissions made to Moll's language additionally substantiate the author's attempt to render her story as realistically as possible. To refer to Mullan's words, "[t]he attachment to the *factual* (however careful a fiction) is what Defoe and Swift exploit" (254). Mullan further notices: "These prefaces are themselves part of the fiction – part of the apparatus of authenticity – just like Swift's publisher's note at the front of *Gulliver's Travels*" (254). In fact, Defoe's "Preface" to *Moll*

---

[41] According to Olsen (2001), the editorial preface should be "loosely as male and specifically as paternalistic" (468).

[42] Rothschild comments upon certain similarities between the preface in Robert Green's *Conversion of an English Courtesan* and Defoe's preface to *Moll Flanders* (Rothschild: 1990 125).

[43] Here is how Davis explains the function of the preface in Defoe's times: "Prefaces to novels in England during the seventeenth and eighteenth century spend a fair amount of time denying this double-fiction. Although the novel seems to be constitutively drawn to the criminal, novelists like Defoe, for example, deny or negate necessity of including 'wicked actions' by saying that these are included only to paint them in 'low-prized colours'" (Defoe, *Roxana*, x). In other words, the criminal content, "Defoe would have us believe, is not inherently part of the novel's discourse, but is only included as an example of behaviour to be reviled" (Davis 1980: 112)

Flanders may serve both to evoke the "forbidden details" in the readers' imagination (Richetti 1975: 197) and to justify any possible inconsistencies in the style and language of the account.

III.3. Realistic (Re)presentation

"The ambition of his fiction is to be fact-like" (Mullan 1998: 255). Saikaku's and Defoe's endeavours to establish the reliability of their narrative voices in some measure explain (or at least imply) why the two writers have been long considered predecessors of realism in Japan and England respectively. It is worth noticing here that the term "realism," coined at the beginning of the 19th century, has been already used in various contexts and is sometimes hastily associated merely with coarseness.[44] In this oversimplified understanding of the term, both *Moll Flanders* and *The Life of an Amorous Woman* may be unequivocally described as "realistic," since they depict the adventures of thieves and prostitutes.

However, as Ian Watt emphasises, "the novel's realism does not reside in the kind of life it presents, but in the way it presents it" (Watt 1957: 11). The term "realism," in this more sophisticated understanding, implies an artistic imitation of reality in all its variety and complexity. A realistic novel should be defined by its attempt to render an individual life in a social and environmental context. In this context, the heroines of the two narratives may be read and interpreted as realistic because they are individuals, colourful examples of ordinary people captured in situations of social conflict, and not because they are roughs.

Apparently, both Saikaku and Defoe present the backgrounds of the "private histories" of their heroines. The Amorous Woman starts her narrative with a reference to her family: "my mother, it is true, was not of noble lineage, but my father was the scion of a gentleman who once enjoyed high rank in the court of the cloistered Emperor Hanazono the Second" (AW 123). In a similar fashion, Moll begins her story by evoking her mother, about whom she knows very little at this point: "my Mother was convicted of Felony for a certain petty Theft scarce worth naming, (*viz.*) Having an opportunity of

---

[44] Ian Watt (1957) claims that "'[r]éalisme' was apparently first used as an aesthetic description in 1835 to denote the 'vérité humaine' of Rembrandt as opposed to the 'idéalité poétique' of neo-classical painting" (9).

borrowing three Pieces of fine *Holland*, of a certain Draper in *Cheapside*" (MF 8). Not only are the two women presented in their social and historical contexts, but their actions are also widely contextualized, indicating the causal relationship between the events depicted in the novels.[45]

The use of detail and meticulous description in the two works may also be seen as one of the realistic techniques employed first by Saikaku and then by Defoe. As one critic claims, "it is the realist novel's concrete details that create its vivid spaces and objects and parallel its individualised characterisations of the novel's protagonist" (Alryyes 2006: 55).[46] It is not uncommon to associate the detailed depiction of everyday life with the realistic novel.

The Life of an Amorous Woman is conspicuous for its descriptions of garments, costumes and fashion accessories: including colourful silk kimonos, stylish sashes, elegant collars, gilt swords, and combs.[47] Similarly, in *Moll Flanders* there are numerous descriptions of the stolen goods, such as "Flanders-Laces," "Gold Watches," "silk Purses of Gold," "full-bottom Periwigs," "silver-fring'd Gloves," and "fine Snuff-boxes" (MF 210, 225).

Moreover, both Saikaku and Defoe frequently focus on the "counting, measuring, pricing, weighing, and evaluating of things in terms of the wealth they represent and the social status they imply for the possessor" (Van Ghent 35). In this way, they render the material world, as well as its cultural and

---

[45] Watt (1957) regards this causal relationship as an important indicator of realism in a novel: "[t]he novel's plot is also distinguished from most previous fiction by its use of past experience as the cause of present action: a causal connection operating through time replaces the reliance of earlier narratives on disguises and coincidences, and this tends to give the novel a much more cohesive structure"(22).

[46] Alryyes thus comments upon Defoe's use of detail: "Defoe's meticulous descriptions, emblematic of the attention he accords to senses, cannot be seen as presaging the accuracy and permanence of a photograph, but as highlighting the uncertain workings of the senses – especially sight – in empirical discourses'"(Alryyes 2006: 67).

[47] Here is an example of Saikaku's descriptive style: "In general their (dancing maidens') form of dress was well determined. Over a red under-kimono lined with silk of the same colour, each girl wore a garment of white padded silk with a pattern embossed in gold and silver foil and a black detachable collar. The sash, which she tied in the back, was of three-coloured cords plaited to the left. By her side the girl would carry a short gilt sword, and she also wore a medicine box and a money pouch. The girls shaved their hair in the middle, so that the forelock was erect like a lad's, and their coiffure stood out in the back; each one, indeed, was the very image of a handsome young man" (AW 126–127).

social implications, and evoke "things" or "res" in Latin, from which the term "realism" derives.[48]

Nonetheless, it does not mean that either Saikaku or Defoe should be unambiguously referred to as "realistic writers."[49] First of all, Saikaku frequently uses poetic stylisation and idealisation of the natural world, which may stem from the fact that traditional Japanese literature did not juxtapose imitation of nature and its beautification (Keene 2001: 89–109). There are also several allusions in Saikaku's novel to the unearthly reality, including to the ghost of the poetess Ono no Komachi or to the apparition of the heroine's unborn children.[50] At one point the woman remembers:

> One night, as I lay gazing into the past through the window of my heart, calling to mind my various wanton doings, I seemed to see a procession of some ninety-five different childlike figures, each child wearing a hat in the form of a lotus leaf and each one stained with blood from his waist down. Standing before me, they spoke in slurred and weeping tones: 'Carry me on your back! Oh, carry me!' (AW 194).

The phantoms of the children in the passage may be interpreted within the context of Japanese tradition of no strict division between the natural and the supernatural.

There are also numerous reservations about Defoe's realism. Some critics claim that the reality he presents is to a large extent already interpreted and therefore biased by his characters.[51] Others emphasise that his picture

---

[48] Skilton (1985) admires Defoe's use of detail in his fiction and non-fiction: "Defoe is a master of circumstantial authenticity. He uses similar techniques in much of his non-fiction too, and in terms of literary methods it is misleading to draw a fast distinction between his factual and his fictional writings" (17).

[49] Karatani (1993) opposes the idea of Saikaku being a realistic writer: "Saikaku was discovered to be a 'realist'. But it is doubtful that Saikaku's writing conformed to our contemporary definition of realism. Saikaku did not 'see things as they are' any more than did Shakespeare, whose dramas were based on classical models and written within the framework of the morality play" (21).

[50] Comp.: "One night, as I lay gazing into the past through the window of my heart, calling to mind my various wanton doings, I seemed to see a procession of some ninety-five different childlike figures, each child wearing a hat in the form of a lotus leaf and each one stained with blood from his waist down. Standing before me, they spoke in slurred and weeping tones: 'Carry me on your back! Oh, carry me!' (AW 194).

[51] Starr (1974) claims that "much of Defoe's rendering of things is not 'factual' or 'referential' at all, but creates this illusion by ascribing to the object qualities which the narrator comes upon, not through simple observation but through process of ego-, ethno- or anthropocentric interpretation. (...) The illusion that the things and events he is describing are real depends to some extent on our not noticing the fundamental artificiality – the 'fictiveness' if

of the world is greatly simplified and reduced to measures and prices. Watt notices, for example, that Defoe is "usually content with denoting only the primary qualities of the objects he describes – their solidity, extension, figure, motion and number – especially number, there is very little attention to the secondary qualities of objects – to their colours, sounds or tastes" (Watt 1957: 102). Preus makes a distinction between the realistic elements in Defoe's fiction and the "traditional divinatory framework," which is used to explain the frequently unfeasible decisions and actions of the characters (460).[52] It thus seems that the persistent critical efforts to associate Defoe with realism must lead unavoidably to the creation of such vague terms as "a little invented realism" (Sutherland 1971: 144).

III.4. Fragmentariness

If the language may serve to enhance the realistic quality of the confession, so may the construction of its plot or the sequence of the events revealed. Watt believes, for example, that in order to present "the life of a real person," it is "recommendable or rather inevitable," to adopt an "episodic but life-like plot sequence" (Watt 1957: 107). It is because the recollections are usually fragmented and incomplete. As a consequence, a genuine confession should be characterised by fragmentariness and inconsistency.

As far as the plots of *The Life of an Amorous Woman* and of *Moll Flanders* are concerned, the narrators pass freely from one episode to another. The choice of the described events often seems random and their importance in the stories varies conspicuously. Sometimes episodes which do not contribute to the overall image of the speaker or which appear tedious are omitted or depicted in a few words. For example, Moll's marriage to Robin, although it lasts five years, is merely mentioned. "Modesty forbids me to reveal the secrets of the marriage-bed," explains Moll, although her modesty

---

not arbitrariness – of his humanising the external world in this way. Nevertheless this illusion is created in part by an essentially symbolic activity, the metaphoric ascription of human traits to external objects" (287).

[52] "So Defoe can be, in part, an author, he can fully exploit his marvellous talent for realistic description in his fiction. But in the 'found' character of his stories, in the critical life-decisions of his characters, and in the lack of evaluative authorial judgements, he remains within the traditional divinatory framework" (Preus 1991: 460).

did not prevent her from indulging in the memories of the advances Robin's brother had made to her earlier.

Similarly, the Amorous Woman focuses on the descriptions of beautiful women, the milieu of the courtesans, and on her own sexual adventures. She passes from the arms of one lover to those of another and craftily hides anything that might have happened in the meantime and does not comply with her image of a passionate and lustful woman.

The fragmentariness of the stories told by the Amorous Woman and Moll is most noticeable in their presentation of other characters. As Watt aptly notices, "although there are some two hundred characters in *Moll Flanders*, no one of them knows the heroine for more than a fraction of her career" (Watt 1957: 112). It appears that most of the characters exist only in relation to Moll's particular adventures. They fade away as soon as she embarks on a new path in her career. In fact, apart from Moll's Lancashire husband and her son, there are hardly any characters that reappear in her life.[53]

The Amorous Woman is even less bound to other characters in the story. She reconciles herself to the death of her first lover with astonishing ease. Never will he reappear in her confession. The presence of other characters is yet more transient. Only the ghosts of her children haunt the woman at night [see above, AW 194, 31–32]. The passage depicts her aborted children and is of great importance in the context of her final repentance.

It seems that in both *The Life of an Amorous Woman* and *Moll Flanders* it is not the logical order but rather the narrators' will that binds the episodes together. The fragmentary quality of their stories is reflected in the way they select and present certain episodes and characters. In this manner, the narrators become the foundation of "the consistency of the tale" (Bell 1985: 155).

There is, however, a noticeable difference in the relationship between the protagonist and the episodes as presented by Saikaku and by Defoe. For Saikaku, the Amorous Woman is the centre of events and simultaneously the pretext for the events. She is a courtesan whose life, by definition, invites erotic adventures. Defoe, on the other hand, endows Moll with a more

---

[53] Sutherland (1971) comments on the significance of the Lancashire husband and Moll's return to Virginia: "In *Moll Flanders* Defoe follows his usual practice of constructing his story in a more or less disconnected series of episodes, of varying length and importance. Some approach to a plot, however, is obtained by the reappearance of Moll's Lancashire husband when she is in Newgate, and by her subsequent return to Virginia, where her second husband and her son are still living on their plantation" (194).

complex personality. He frequently uses the episodes to reveal something important about her. As a consequence, some critics postulate reading Defoe "as a novelist of character rather than of incident" (Brown 1996: 313). This, however debatable (there is more than one incident in Moll's story which does not disclose anything about her personality), helps in understanding Moll as not subordinate to the episodes she narrates, which is often the case with the Amorous Woman.

Importantly, the episodic structure of the two confessions does not entail a lack of development. Saikaku's protagonist follows one erotic adventure after another to finally hit bottom, and to be led to repentance and confession. The fact that she ages is also of some consequence in the whole process. Defoe's Moll, on the other hand, makes "successive attempts to achieve ... a respectable and secure position" (Hühn 2001: 337). She develops towards personal independence and social stability.[54] In her case, repentance is not the final stage but it helps her achieve a better position in society. In this context, we may agree that her story has "all the structure of a traditional Christian experience" (Koonce 1963: 384).

III.5. The Reader Who Witnesses

The audience is as much an integral part of any confession as the writer/speaker and the message. Since it has already been established that the writer/speaker should be above all trustworthy and the message should be a revelation of the past experiences (preferably mysterious ones), it might be interesting now to consider the role of the reader/listener in the entire process.

In *The Life on an Amorous Woman* it is the male narrator – an anonymous youth – who becomes the listener to the woman's story. On his journey he meets two other travellers who attract his attention: the first is "so languid, wan and gaunt from love that his survival seemed precarious and one could but judge that he would soon depart this world" (AW 121); the other open-

---

[54] Dannenberg (2004) does not focus on Moll's proceeding from "insecurity to social stability but rather on the process of her gaining self-knowledge," claiming that "[i]n the history of narrative fiction, Defoe's *Moll Flanders* provides an innovative example of suspense generation within the coincidence plot, in which staggered recognition and a long deferral between partial and full recognition creates suspense on both the character-cognitive and the readerly levels" (416).

ly expresses his wish to "find a country without women" (AW 121). The male narrator decides to follow the bizarre travellers and, thus, he reaches a secluded place where "the red pine trees grew in clusters" (AW 122). This is the place where the Amorous Woman finds her shelter from the outside world and where she tells her story to anybody who is eager to listen.

It is necessary to acknowledge that the readers of *The Life of an Amorous Woman* (and the listeners to the woman's story) knew the world of pleasures represented in the work. The listeners experienced it and now they either long for it or they seek shelter from it. The Amorous Woman welcomes everybody with the same coquettish courtesy:

> So you have come today to visit me once more. Surely the world is full of alluring girls with whom young gentlemen like you might dally! Why, then, does the fresh wind blow on this withered tree? I have of late become hard of hearing, nor can I any longer express myself with ease…Why, good sirs, do you come to visit me? (AW 123).

The woman greets the readers of her story in the same manner as she welcomes her guests. Similarly, the readers enter the company of the travellers and repeat their request: "Having heard, madam, of your great repute, we have come here to learn these mysteries from you. Pray tell us afresh of your own rich past" (AW 123). The woman's confession thus stems from her desire both to be relieved and to please everybody by responding to their enquiries about the realm of earthly love.

In *The Life of an Amorous Woman* the readers may identify themselves with the visitors to the courtesan's shelter; in *Moll Flanders* they are spoken to directly. If there is any intermediary between the readers and Moll, it is the editor or the author of the preface. It is in the preface that the ideal reader of Defoe's book is suggested:

> But as this Work is chiefly recommended to those who know how to Read it, and how to make the good Uses of it, which the Story all along recommends to them; so it is to be hop'd that such Readers will be more pleas'd with the Moral, than the Fable; with the Application than with the Relation, and with the End of the Writer, than with the Life of the Person written of (MF 2).

Moll's story is addressed not so much to a specific person or to a certain group of people (as is the case with Saikaku's work) but rather to a general audience or to anybody familiar with life in eighteenth-century England. Nonetheless, as the editor indicates, it is also important that the reader focuses not on the pleasing qualities of Moll's account but on its moral implications. This idea expressed in the preface proves that Defoe's books might have been "a kind of conscience," "meant to work in a public mind" (Preston 1970: 8).

The fact that the reader of *Moll Flanders* is not specified influences the story as much as the way in which it is told. Moll speaks about her life and past secrets in a manner that is as neutral as possible. To what extent the style of her account is shaped by the editor is a question that, of course, cannot be answered easily. Nonetheless, it appears that she attempts to provide a "medium in which the reader can face himself" (Preston 1970: 37). She appeals to any reader who can be sympathetic to her story.

III.6. Didactic Purpose

Since the confession usually means the disclosure of the speaker's trespasses, it has an unavoidably didactic purpose woven into it. The ethical aspect of a confessional narrative is two-dimensional as it concerns both the speaker/writer and the listener/reader. Both the Amorous Woman and Moll are eager to confess their secrets because they want to be relieved from the burden of the past. Their stories are addressed to the readers, for whom they set an example of moral behaviour and whom they discourage from wrongful deeds. However, in the case of Saikaku's work, the didacticism may be questioned as the convention of Buddhist confession borders on parody (Hibbett 1957: 67). The speaker's pleasure derived from recalling her past mischief is sometimes too pungent to be easily reconciled with her declared grief.

III.7. Crime and Guilt

Moll's confession is inspired by Christian tradition of expressing guilt and of repentance, which results in redemption. This is because "the world of Defoe ... was based on religious presuppositions" (Rogers 1978: 118).[55] Not

---

[55] Strange (1976) also focuses on the importance of Defoe's religious underpinning: "If we can understand and accept Defoe's notion of what man is, how man thinks and how he relates to God and his world – in other words his Calvinistic beliefs – we can read the work as Chalmers did and how Defoe wrote it" (153).

only in *Moll Flanders* but also in his other works "does [Defoe] stress the possibility of the ultimate redemption through repentance" (CS[56] x).

In this context, Moll's decision to begin with describing her innocent childhood and only then tell the story of her mischief may be interpreted as a parallel to the Biblical story of Adam and Eve, and of the whole human race. As Bishop (1952) notices, "the artistic pattern of the novel is the same as the moral pattern of history according to Calvinist theology" (13). Moll, truly a representative of the human race, proceeds from "primal innocence through the guilt of experience to salvation; starts as a culpable Adam and ends redeemed by Christ" (Bishop 1952: 13).

The notion of Original Sin may also be traced in Moll's account. Just as Eve disobeyed God's order and thus found herself and all her future off-spring banished from the Garden of Eden, Moll's mother committed crimes which later condemned Moll to life as a thief. It is not a coincidence then that Moll begins her story by referring both to her mother and to Newgate:

> My Mother was convicted of Felony … she was call'd Down, as they term it, to her former Judgment, but obtain'd the Favour of being Transported to the Plantations, and left me about Half a Year old; and in bad Hands, you may be sure (MF 8).

The tone of the passage is ominous. It suggests that Moll's later conduct was predetermined by her mother's crime. Even Moll's alias – "Flanders" – evokes the "pieces of fine Holland" her mother stole. Watt emphasises the re-ligious determination of the protagonist who tries to perceive "the mundane events of the narrative as divine pointers which may help him to find his own place in the eternal scheme of redemption and reprobation" (Watt 1957: 77). Similarly, the way in which Moll tries to interpret her reality in terms of the moral message it should convey, may point to a Puritan perspective. In this context, it is possible to say that Defoe's work indeed operates "within the framework of puritan theology" (CS ix). As a consequence, Moll's mother becomes the Eve figure who has doomed her own children.

The sense of quilt is not explored by Saikaku as his protagonist moves and speaks within the conventions of *gesaku* writings embodying the aes-thetic values of *ukiyo*. In fact, the lack of quilt is also understandable in the context of *zange* tradition. Childs convincingly explains that "although forgiveness is said to be one of the root meanings of *zange*, the sense of the

---

[56] *Captain Singleton.*

term in the context of revelatory tales by no means involves the feeling of guilt found in the Christian practice of confession or repentance of sins" (56). The Amorous Woman is much eager to reveal her story and much less keen to repent.

III.8. Providence

The confession of Moll Flanders cannot be interpreted without referring to the notion of Providence initiating and shaping her life in the novel. It is possible to say that the goal of the novel is "to find the factual 'particulars' that make a narrative individual – and thence the shapes of providential design (…) amidst all the details" (Mullan 1998: 257). Naturally, Defoe's attempt to indicate how Providence operated in Moll's life was not unnoticed by his contemporaries. Charles Gildon even denounced him on the basis that "the Christian religion and the doctrines of providence are too sacred to be delivered in fictions and lies" (Davis 1980: 117).

Paradoxically, Providence in *Moll Flanders* often operates by means of coincidence or mere chance, which some critics explain by emphasising Defoe's interest in "lotteries and games of chance" (Hentzi 1991: 192).[57] It is by coincidence that Moll encounters her mother in Virginia, although this encounter does make Moll realise the incestuous character of her marriage. The readers cannot but associate this episode with Moll's previous relation to the Colchester Brothers, which she herself considered incestuous. In this manner, the repetitiveness of Moll's fate is made even more noticeable. Moreover, it is interesting how luck may be easily associated in *Moll Flanders* with Providence. Whenever Moll is successful, be it in gambling or marriage, it can be "reducible to her favour with God" (Novak 1963: 7). In this context, the successful conclusion of Moll's confession may also indicate the final approval of God.

If Providence sometimes relies on coincidence to shape Moll's life, it also uses nature to the extent that it "is often indistinguishable from nature" (Novak 1963: 6).[58] Hence, many natural reasons are given in order to explain

---

[57] Hentzi (1991) also refers to Defoe's pamphlet "The Gamester. No. II" which is on the subject of chance and its significance (191).

[58] Hühn (2001) speaks about Moll's tendency to search for meaning in the environment: "The specific modality of her second-order self-observation consists in observing herself as

Moll's lot. In the end, however, it is God who is the "final cause" (Novak 1963: 7). In this respect, the message conveyed in *Moll Flanders* is far more meditative and introspective than that of *The Life of an Amorous Woman*.[59] It is because Saikaku focuses on the simple joys of the floating world (*ukiyo*). Even if he realises at the very beginning that "death is the fate that no one can escape" (AW 121), he lets his protagonist drift around earthly pleasures as long as possible.

III.9. Virtue and Vice

The narrative distance (in both time and space) of the Amorous Woman and Moll enables them to make more general comments upon life, virtue and vice. These comments are frequently at odds with the protagonists' behaviour but they also prove that didactic purpose was not unimportant for either Saikaku or Defoe.[60]

The narrator of *The Life of an Amorous Woman*, external to the story-world, sometimes stigmatises the wickedness of jealousy, claiming that "nothing in this world is as fearful as a woman's jealousy, be she high-born or of low estate" (AW 135–136) or that "truly, jealousy is a thing to be eschewed, and we women must ever guard ourselves against it" (AW 172). Moreover, the narrator complains that "in this Floating World we cannot have everything as we wish. But when a man can choose between two women, it is always the fairer who will win" (AW 173).

There are likewise several remarks incorporated in the main body of Moll's narrative which criticise the vices of the world, but where Saikaku blames humans for their jealousy, Defoe accuses the devil.[61] As a conse-

---

being observed by God. Thus, she is able to attribute the meaningfulness of her life-story to the environment rather than to her own activity" (338).

[59] Hentzi (1991) emphasizes that depending on Providence is typical of the "religious forms of self-examination" (193). Strange (1976) reads *Moll Flanders* as a serious religious work: "As the work of a Calvinist in the eighteenth century Defoe's *Moll Flanders* is a seriously conceived, philosophically consistent, and psychologically sound artistic production" (154).

[60] "This was a problem which was to run through all Defoe's works. As he saw it, a writer had a double obligation to entertain and to instruct, but of the two instruction was the most important. In 1704 he compared the responsibilities of the writer and the preacher" (Earle 1973: 31).

[61] Earle (1973) comments upon the function of the devil in Defoe's writings: "The Devil was just as real as God to Defoe. Indeed, the evidence for his existence lay in the existence of God" (36).

quence, in most cases not Moll but the devil is considered responsible for the wickedness of her actions. She tends to consider "the devil as the perpetrator" and to "see herself as a passive victim, her mind distracted and her body at the mercy of outside forces beyond her control" (Rabin 2003: 95). At one point, for example, Defoe puts into Moll's mouth a general remark: "as the Devil is an unwearied Tempter, so he never fails to find opportunity for that Wickedness he invites to" (MF 26).

Moreover, throughout her story Moll emphasises that poverty is the devil's most effective instrument, one used to compel people (including herself) to act wickedly: "the Devil never fails to excite us to from the frightful prospect of Poverty and Distress" (MF 125). She even equates the devil with poverty: "I, prompted by that worst of Devils, Poverty, return'd to the vile Practice, and made the Advantage of what they call a handsome Face, be the Relief to my Necessities, and Beauty be a Pimp to Vice" (MF 188).[62] Undoubtedly, Moll's views on the roots of all evil in the world may be associated with the Calvinist concept of predestination, the belief that human beings are not in a position to act entirely of their free will.

III.10. Signs of Repentance

Despite the considerable lack of a moral message in Saikaku's work, both the Amorous Woman and Moll make attempts to express their self-criticism while narrating the stories of their lives. Saikaku's protagonist admits, for example, that her conduct was "terrible":

> As I stood there gazing calmly at these five hundred Buddhas, I found that every single one reminded me of some man with whom in the past I had been intimate. I thought back incident by incident on all my years in the sad floating trade, and felt that nothing in the world is so terrible as a woman who practises this calling (AW 206–207).

---

[62] Here is how Earle (1973) explains Defoe's use of poverty (i.e. necessity) as an excuse for crime: "Defoe does not deny that the sin committed as a result of necessity is still a sin but he argues that the necessity which caused it is sufficient grounds for tolerance and forgiveness on the part of society. He often goes farther than this, blaming society for the poverty which led to the sin in the first place" (36).

And she adds:

My breast seemed to roar like the chariot of fire and tears welled up in my eyes like bubbles of boiling water. I was overcome by a delirium of grief, and quite forgetting that I was in a temple, I fell down to the ground (AW 207).

She depicts her grief in an exaggerated, although not entirely unconvincing, manner. She even makes reference to Buddhist Hell as she speaks about the "chariot of fire" (*hi no kuruma*) which was believed to carry wrongdoers to tortures and nowadays is a symbol of dire poverty or misfortunes.

Moll Flanders even more openly expresses her grief and repentance: "I repented heartily of all my Life past" (MF 274). Contrary to Saikaku's Amorous Woman, she analyses her motivation as a penitent, reflecting upon her grief:

[A]ll my Repentance appear'd to me to be only the effect of my fear of Death, not a sincere regret for the wicked Life that I had liv'd, and which had brought this Misery upon me, for the offending of my Creator, who was now suddenly to be my Judge (MF 277).

Moll distinguishes between the "fear of death" and genuine "repentance" after having offended God.[63] Contrarily, the Amorous Woman does not even consider such a distinction. Her repentance stems from her fear of Buddhist Hell and tortures.

The question of repentance is not, however, easily resolved in either of the two works. Although the women express their grief, most of the time they indulge in the recollections of their own trespasses. Neither the Amorous Woman nor Moll is really consistent or convincing in their repentance.[64] The Amorous Woman tends to emphasise her pleasures and sexual enjoyment rather than sincere remorse for her behaviour. Though she is already not long for this world, she even remembers with regret the moments when she lay in bed alone: "as I lay in bed sunk in reverie, it occurred to me that to sleep alone as I now did was a sorry thing indeed" (AW 178).

---

[63] Critics agree that it is rather the fear of punishment that motivates Moll: "Moll Flanders' repentance in the condemned cell at Newgate was at first no better that that of Roxana, being based only on the fear of death" (Earl 1973: 278).

[64] Watt (1957) comments on the lack of coherent moral message in *Moll Flanders*: "Defoe, then, failed to locate his didactic commentary convincingly in any particular period of his heroine's moral development; and this may stand as an example of his general failure to resolve the formal problems to which his moral purpose and his autobiographical narrative mode committed him" (117).

On the other hand, Moll admits to her pride and greed as she yearns for "one Booty more that might compleat my Desires" (MF 207). Nonetheless, she also admits that "thou' I certainly had that one Booty, yet every hit look'd towards another, and was so encouraging to me to go on with the Trade" (MF 207). She confesses again: "things were a Temptation to me, that I was poor, and distress'd, and between, and Poverty was what many cou'd not resist" (MF 274).[65]

Moreover, throughout her story Moll seems rather proud than ashamed of her thieving achievements. She draws an "obvious pleasure" from "some of her criminal activities" and her language, according to the editor, happens to be "offensive" (Novak 1983: 60). As a consequence, Moll's account of her crimes is full of self-importance. Even when she steals a necklace from an innocent child she focuses on her own wits and cunning:

> The Child had a little Necklace on of Gold Beads, and I had my Eye upon that, and in the dark of the Alley I stoop'd, pretending to mend the Child's Clog that was loose, and took off her Necklace, and the Child never felt it, and so led the Child on again (MF 194).

Undoubtedly, this passage illustrates what Birdsall calls Moll's "pride in her artistry" (Birdsall 96). It does not necessarily undermine the protagonist's final repentance, although it does indicate a certain incongruity in her behaviour.

The act of repentance is questioned also in *The Life of an Amorous Woman*. One of the moments when the narrator speaks about the need for forgiveness is when she deceives one of her lovers, telling him that she is sixteen. At this point she reflects upon her act of deception:

> Fortunately it was dark and he could not see me in my true form. But since I am, in fact, fifty-eight, I had told him a lie of forty-two years! When I reach the next world, I shall surely be censured by the devil and even have my tongue pulled out for my deceit. I only hope that he may forgive me by taking into account that this is my only way to earn a living (MF 199–200).

The purpose of her story is to inspire astonishment that in her age she could have been mistaken for such young girl, and although she speaks of

---

[65] Skilton (1985) also claims that Moll's repentance may be unconvincing due to her enumerations of profits: "Because of Moll Flanders' loving catalogues of her gains, her account of her own repentance does not convincingly add up to an improving moral tale: her moralising sits too lightly on her throughout her story" (14).

the possibility of future punishment she recalls the event with pride and emphasises that she was forced to lead a life of deception. Her narration should also be viewed in the light of what she says about confession early in the story when she exposes her affair with her master:

> [B]y revealing my deceits and my full shame, I exposed my master to grievous scandal. Truly, to disclose at a stroke all the wantonness of one's past months and years is a thing that anyone in this world must guard against (AW 164).

From that moment her attitude to confession becomes pragmatic. No wonder then that she starts her confession only after she has realised that she is sheltered from its consequences.

We might argue that both Saikaku and Defoe are sometimes "better at the entertainment than at conveying the moral" and their "habit of illustrating the vice which (they were) condemning gradually took over from the condemnation itself" (Earle 1973: 32). It is because they loved above all "to contemplate human life" (Sutherland 1971: 246). Moreover, since they were both brought up among artisans, they were very much interested in the technique itself.[66] As Sutherland (1971) comments upon Defoe's attitude to his characters' skills, "how things were done … always fascinated him far more than what was going on inside people's heads" (247). Both the Amorous Woman and Moll thus become the "greatest artists" of their times (Novak 1963: 83): the former as a courtesan, the latter as a thief.

Finally, if we decide to reflect upon the sincerity of repentance as expressed by the two women, it should not be overlooked that they are always speaking to someone. The audience plays an important role in their moral message and in the way they present it. Although they claim that they are repentant confessors, they also tend to make, as Koonce (1963) phrased it in reference to Moll, "an amazingly self-confident appeal for sympathy" (381). They focus on their difficult position in life and call for a compassionate reception.

---

[66] Brown (1996) speaks about the inherent dichotomy in Defoe's works of fiction: "on the one hand, the imperative of explicit moral didacticism, not integrated as ethical choice, and on the other, pleasure, but not an aesthetic pleasure, in the artifice of the well-made plot" (313–314).

Chapter IV. Intricacies of Confessional Narrative

The confessional narrative involves a number of fundamental tensions between concealment and disclosure, detachment and involvement, experience and inexperience, past and present. On the one hand, the confessors express their innermost feelings and experiences, kept secret for a long time. On the other, they make a courageous attempt to reveal them to the audience. Consequently, the speaker inevitably adopts a double function in the story: of both narrator and protagonist.

IV.1. Between Concealment and Disclosure

It is worth noticing that the narrators in both novels remain anonymous from the outset of the events till the very end. Saikaku's heroine, referred to as *Kōshoku Ichidai Onna* ("One Amorous Woman"), does not even mention her name to the listeners (and readers) of her story, while Defoe's Moll Flanders uses various aliases or generic names (e.g. Betty, a typical name for maidservants in the eighteenth century England).[67]

The Amorous Woman first appears in the novel as *rōjo* ("an old lady") and, in this manner, begins her confession, throughout which she keeps her name entirely secret. The Japanese grammar, characterised by frequent omissions of personal pronouns, contributes to the successful concealment of the heroine's name.

In *Moll Flanders*, on the other hand, the editor introduces the heroine and the main narrator as early as in the "Preface" as "this famous *Moll Flanders*, as she calls herself" (MF 5), thus indicating that the name is invented by the heroine for the sake of the narrative. Later, Moll (her surname stemming

---

[67] On the subject of the use of generic names in *Moll Flanders* see: Watt 1949: 322–323; Chaber 1982: 212.

from the Flemish lace)[68] bids the readers to accept her alias under which she was known to her fellow thieves: "so you may give me leave to speak of myself under that Name till I dare own who I have been, as well as who I am" (MF 7).

If the names of the narrators are shrouded in mystery, so are the names of many other characters who are frequently described in terms of their relation to others, i.e. "Elder Brother," "a highwayman" and "Lancashire husband" in *Moll Flanders*, or "a provincial Lord" and "my master" in *The Life of an Amorous Woman*. In fact, it is the prevailing tendency to conceal names that forces the readers to "refer to the characters by their personal relationships to one another" (Olsen 2001: 477).

It seems that the strong tendency to obscure the narrators' names and the names of their acquaintances is purposeful and artistically most effective. In this way the narrators manage to create an undisturbed sphere necessary for private confession. They also reconstruct the actual anonymity which also protected them from the world at the time they performed their morally and socially unacceptable or dubious deeds.

Contrary to Saikaku, who in many of his other works makes successful use of factual, historic names, for example in *Five Woman Who Loved Love*, Defoe frequently uses aliases in his confessional fiction. Perhaps he believed that they granted far more freedom of expression to the speakers.[69] Except for Robinson Crusoe, not many of his narrators reveal their true names to the readers. Rather, like Roxana or Captain Singleton, they speak under nicknames. Nonetheless, their nicknames sound very plausible and could be often mistaken for the names of real people, which according to Ian Watt is characteristic of "the professedly non-fictional 'true histories,' biographies and memoirs" (Watt 1949: 322).

Whilst Moll uses various aliases to hide her true identity, the anonymous Amorous Woman throughout the story adopts various guises depending on the circumstances she happens to be in. When she wants to join the company of Buddhist monks, she shaves her head "in the centre to look like a young man's" and puts on a "man's loincloth" (AW 148). She even fakes a man's voice in order to take on the semblance of a young masterless samurai, be-

---

[68] Rebecca Connor (2004) claims that Moll's nickname indicates that the "price of a commodity has both intrinsic and extrinsic meaning for Moll's self" (111).

[69] Brown (1971) draws a parallel between the nicknames of Defoe's narrator and his own aliases which he frequently used as a political writer and polemist (563).

lieving that such camouflage would enable her to move out and about "even at noon, without hiding from [other] people" (Nenzi 2008: 99). At another occasion, as a supervisor of courtesans, she wears "a light-mauve apron and a sash of medium width, tied on the left side" (AW 192) and adopts a fearsome look. The anonymity is made possible by the character of *ukiyo*, as Berry (2006) aptly notices:

> In a "drifting world," city people crossed paths as newcomers, tourists, pilgrims, shoppers, and seekers. And they shared sufferings and pleasures: love, debt, swaggering superiors, ready entertainment, escape into anonymity (34).

Similarly, Moll Flanders, once she enters the path of thievery, survives in London only by adopting a variety of disguises and hiding her true identity even from her companions and accomplices. By concealing the real and dramatic consequences of her action from herself, Moll manages to survive not only physically but also "psychologically" (Birdsall 1985: 91).[70] She hides from herself the effects of her wrongdoing and thus succeeds in keeping her integrity as a human being.

Both Moll Flanders and the Amorous Woman use disguise effectively in order to build up the tension necessary for their stories revolving around mystery and its revelation. In this manner, the narrators tell their tales under a "double compulsion to expose and to conceal themselves" (Brown 1971: 562). Paradoxically, they hide their names, important emblems of their identity, in order to continue revealing their private histories.

It is worth remembering that the women not only manage to withhold their true names but they are also successful in hiding other information about their lives. Of course, some details of their past (e.g. the details concerning Moll's mother) are unknown to them at the point of time which they want to reconstruct in their narration. Nonetheless, they are very careful not to reveal too much and often choose to draw a veil over some episodes either to attract the reader's attention or to appeal to their sympathy.[71]

---

[70] Richard Burton (1909) notices Defoe's attempts at a psychological depiction but concludes "Defoe and Swift may be said to have added some slight interest in analysis pointing towards the psychologic method, which was to find full expression in Samuel Richardson" (47).

[71] Birdsall (1985) thus comments on Moll's confession: "Certainly, she does withhold information from her readers. If most of the people in her life do not know who she really is, neither do her readers ever really know. To tell us would be to take a chance on giving too much away" (90).

IV.2. Between Detachment and Involvement

This double function of the speaker in the confessional narrative is detectable in both *The Life of an Amorous Woman* and *Moll Flanders*. The two women relate the episodes of their lives from a distance of both time and space, which should prove their stories to be objective and reliable. Nonetheless, they are also involved in the events they retell. However detached from the past they might be, they are at the same time strongly influenced by the passions and indignations associated with their own experiences and retained in their memories. As a consequence, they seem to be "analytical, reflective, judicious" on the one hand, and "instinctive, panicky, muddled" on the other (Rogers 1974: 264).

One of the earliest episodes in *The Life of an Amorous Woman*, concerned with the death of the narrator's first lover, craftily renders the tension between the woman's passion of a moment and her narrative distance:

> My lover, most grievous to relate, was put to death. For some days thereafter, as I lay tossing on my bed, half asleep, half awake, his silent form would appear terrifyingly before me. In my agony I thought that I must needs take my own life; yet, after some days had passed, I completely forgot about him. From this one may truly judge that nothing in this world is as base and fickle as a woman's heart (AW 125).

The woman juxtaposes the despair and suffering after her lover's death with the ephemeral quality of her own love. In one moment she remembers how she wished to die, in another she declares that she forgot her pain in no less than a few days. Additionally, she makes a general comment on the nature of women as volatile and untrustworthy.

The Amorous Woman is especially artful at rendering momentary sexual desire. Although she describes her erotic adventures with detachment from the distance of her hermitage and of her old age, her account is amazingly vivid and evocative:

> One night while I lay in lonely wakefulness, the gentleman's leg touched my body. All other thoughts now left my head as I listened with pricked ears for the sound of the lady's snores. Being assured, then, that she slept, I crept under her husband's bedclothes and set about seducing him. Soon we were both transported with our single-minded lust (AW 129).

The passage truly appeals to the senses of touch and hearing. In fact, it reflects the sudden single-mindedness of the passionate heroine. It is only later, when the woman speaks about the consequences of her behaviour ("Thus was I once again sent back to my parents' home," AW 129), that she adheres again to her role of a story-teller.

In a similar fashion, Moll Flanders oscillates throughout her account between the narrative distance and the emotional involvement in the narrated events. The depiction of the process of her being seduced by the elder brother may well exemplify her double role in the story:

> [The elder brother] 'briskly comes up the Stairs and, seeing me at Work, comes into the Room to me directly, and began just as he did before, with taking me in his Arms, and Kissing me for almost a quarter of an Hour together (MF 23).

The use of the present tense emphasises Moll's emotional involvement in the episode and intensifies the sensuous appeal of the whole scene. Her participation, naturally, does not mean that she necessarily initiates the action itself, and she is often the object of the advances of others. While possessing "an active intelligence which transforms itself to meet the needs of experience," Moll is simultaneously "the passive entity to which the incidents happen" (Richetti 1975: 101). At the end of the passage, however, Moll-the-participant gives way to Moll-the-narrator, as she recounts her passionate encounter with stunning precision.

In another passage referring to her relationship with the elder brother, Moll admits that she was mistaken in her immature judgement of the situation: "the Mistake lay here, that Mrs. *Betty* was in Earnest and the Gentleman was not" (MF 22). Here, the narrative distance is indicated by the use of expressions: "Mrs. Betty" (indicating the narrator in her youth and inexperience) and "the gentleman" (referring to the elder brother). Furthermore, the term "gentleman," apart from indicating the social position of the man, is obviously used in an ironic sense to highlight the brother's dishonesty and deception. As Novak (1996) rightly notices, "[t]he split between the wise, experienced female narrator and the young Moll seems to make everything possible" (57).

Not only does Moll frequently reveal her lover's true self, but she also muses upon her own less than decent intentions and discloses them to the readers with utmost honesty:

> I had a most unbounded Stock of Vanity and Pride, and but a very little Stock of Virtue. I did indeed case sometimes with myself what young Master aim'd at, but

thought of nothing but the fine Words and the Gold; whether he intended to Marry me, or not to Marry me, seemed a matter of no great Consequence to me (MF 25).[72]

Moll's insightful interpretation of her own motives and reactions proves that although she "has lived life for the moment," she is able and even eager at times to tell "her story with detached comprehension" (Rogers 1974: 266). In this way, she manages to function both "as a memorialist and as an active person" (Piper 1969: 501).

IV.3. Between Past and Present

Since confession is a very complex process of uncovering the past and relocating it in the present, the narrated events seem to exist both in years gone by and in the here and now of the story-teller. There are, therefore, numerous complications with regard to the time and its representation in the story. On the one hand, the narrator attempts to render the past events in as coherent a manner as possible. On the other, she is strongly influenced by the present moment in and through which the story is told. Moreover, although the narration is presented "from the vantage-point of the end" (Hühn 2001: 400), it also evokes particular moments from the past.

In both *The Life of an Amorous Woman* and *Moll Flanders* the narrators choose linear representation of their stories, as they attempt to retell the events in chronological order. The woman in Saikaku's novel first tells of her parents and family background and then proceeds to describe the subsequent years of her life.

In a similar fashion, Moll starts with recounting the obscure circumstances of her birth and then continues, evoking her more distinct memories in sequence: "[t]he first Account that I can recollect, or could ever learn of myself, was that I had wandered among a Crew of those people they call *gypsies*, or *Egyptians*" (MF 9). The opening of the narratives may, therefore,

---

[72] The Amorous Woman also confesses her own hypocrisy: "From this time forward I was seamstress in name only. I took my pleasure here and there, having set my fee at one rectangular gold piece a day. Though I had the maid carry my workbox when I went out on my visits, it was by another form of work that I contrived to make my living; for, as one might say, the thread with which I now so loosely sewed would not serve for binding buttocks" (AW 183). The indecent character of her "visits" is emphasised by the Japanese proverb: *shiri o musubanu* ("not binding the buttocks").

suggest a diachronic presentation of the heroines' lives. However, the past is also coexistent with and influenced by the present.

The here and now of the narrators is indicated in the beginning of the narratives. The Amorous Woman is already presented in the first chapter as an elderly lady and a humble penitent recounting her adventures in love to the nameless listeners. She even emphasises her own old age: "I have of late become hard of hearing, nor can I any longer express myself with ease" (AW 123). She also compares herself to a withered tree.

Not only does she indicate her decrepit age, paralleled by the ragged landscape that surrounds her, but she also suggests its influence on her storytelling.[73] Similarly, she anticipates the audacious character of her past conduct: "I did not begin life in my present humble state" (AW 123). The reader may then suppose that her penitent role in the present may have its effect on her story, too.

Moll Flanders is also introduced as a repentant woman. First the author foretells her "foolish, Thoughtless, and abhorr'd Conduct" (MF 2) and admits that she has "grown Penitent and Humble, as she afterwards pretends to be" (MF 1). Then, Moll herself confesses that she was "brought into a Course of Life which was not only scandalous in itself, but which in its ordinary Course tended to the swift Destruction both of Soul and Body" (MF 8). In this way, she evaluates her past from the perspective of her cosy and repentant present. Thus, the beginning of her confession signals the frequent fusion (and confusion) of time. It also underlines the synchronic quality of the story.[74]

The coexistence of past and present in *Moll Flanders* may also be exemplified by the use of the historical present tense.[75] The *praesens historicum* is especially frequent in Moll's description of the scenes of her seduction by the elder brother. She notices at one point: "[H]e comes in with an Air of gayty. O! Mrs. *Betty*, said he to me, how do you do, Mrs. *Betty*? Don't your

---

[73] "A tablet, wrought of a piece of bleached wood, hung from the lintel of the chamber where she evidently slept at night, and on it appeared the device, 'The Cell of Love.' A lingering aroma hovered in the air; I judged it to be that incense called 'First Music' of which I had heard people speak" (AW 122).

[74] "Defoe's world is always synchronic rather than diachronic. The past is imported into the present as a psychological re-creatable state. Hence Moll's reactions are indeed confused and ambiguous" (Novak 1970: 364)

[75] Monika Fludernik (2003) discusses the representation of time and the use of *praesens historicum* in *Moll Flanders* (124).

cheeks burn, Mrs. *Betty*?" (MF 20). Both the tense and the repetition of the man's direct words manifest not only Moll's capacity as a narrator but also her eagerness to relive her own past in the present. For a moment, Moll-the speaker becomes again the young and inexperienced "Mrs Betty."[76]

The combination of the synchronic and diachronic representation of time in the two stories has its influence on the pace at which the events are reported. In *The Life of an Amorous Woman* the story is frequently delayed by elaborate descriptions of costumes and ornaments which render the atmosphere of different places and reflect the social status of the characters. Moreover, the woman often refers to *kigo*, traditional expressions evocative of the seasons, and to famous poems depicting nature or encounters of lovers. This opens the narrative to a broader analysis in the context of Japanese poetics and aesthetics. The following passage may illustrate this tendency:

> In the great park the Kirishima azaleas had come into bloom, and all the fields and hills were decked in crimson; crimson too were the trousers that the ladies-in-waiting wore as they moved about softly on their *kemari* shoes, indulging in divers pretty plays like Cherry-Piling and Mountain-Crossing. They had hung their robes on the bamboo hedge and the wide sleeves were fluttering in the breeze (AW 164–165).

The azalea flowers (*tsutsuji*), especially beautiful in the region of Kirishima in Kagoshima on Kyūshū, are mentioned here to evoke spring with all its colours and fragrance. The crimson colour (*kurenai*) merges the image of petals with that of garments in a poetic manner, typical of *haikai* poetry. Moreover, the *kemari* shoes metonymically bring the image of the traditional theatrical performance in the open air (*kemari*). In this manner, the Amorous Woman savours the past moments of her life while allowing reader to savour her descriptions.

The pace of *Moll Flanders* is much less leisurely than that of Saikaku's work.[77] Moll appears to leap from one relationship into another, from one place to another, from one technique of survival to another. She meets

---

[76] This incorporation of the interior voice into the exterior narrative is precisely what Hühn (2001) would call a "simultaneous interior focalisation" (400). Goldknopf (1969) emphasises Moll's joy in retelling and reliving certain events of her life: "what is true of certain details in the story is, in a sense, true of the entire work, since presented as a cautionary tale, *Moll Flanders* is really Moll's way of reliving her illicit pleasures and triumphs in the mellowness of her waning years" (21).

[77] Critics generally agree on the brisk pace of *Moll Flanders*: "*Moll Flanders* has been attacked for its multiplicity of adventures, yet one chap book version managed to squeeze them all into eight pages. Surely no story teller ever told his tale at the pace of Conrad's Marlowe; neither did anyone ever tell a story at Moll Flanders' pace" (Novak 1973: 131).

numerous characters on her way, most of whom do not reappear, travels to distant places and tries to sustain herself in most hazardous ways. The brisk pace invites the readers to participate in her experience rather than merely to contemplate it (Bishop 1952: 3).

Although some critics claim that Moll Flanders's manner of telling is "dry" and "seriatim" (Rogers 1974: 263), the pace of her story nonetheless varies conspicuously. There are moments when she deliberately pauses either to attract the readers' attention or to emphasise her economic situation and the artistry of her "profession." Moll's description of her seduction by the elder brother is one example of her tempting and seducing the reader. As Olsen (2001) realises: "The elder brother's sexual desire and enjoyment lie in delay, and both the editor and Moll seduce the reader by delaying her actual seduction" (472). The narration reflects or adjusts to the duration and significance of the narrated events.

Most of Moll's narrative "pauses," however, refer to her finances. For example, after her husband Jemmy leaves her, she considers the money matters in great detail: "I felt in my Pocket, and there found ten Guineas, his Gold Watch, and two little Rings, one a small Diamond Ring worth only about £6, and the other a plain Gold Ring" (MF 153). This demonstrates the extent to which an independent woman had to think about her income in order to survive in eighteenth-century English society. It also illustrates Moll's materialistic approach to life.

The question of narrative pace is related to the problem of selection and omissions made by a story-teller whose focus is usually suggested by the amount of time devoted to particular descriptions. In the case of *The Life of an Amorous Woman* and *Moll Flanders* priority is given to the amorous and thievish adventures of the heroines. As a consequence, all "dull and domestic" episodes (Bell 1985: 162) are craftily omitted. The Amorous Woman's mourning after the death of her lover fades away within "some days" (AW 125). Moreover, Moll's marriage to Robin is described in a few lines "with indecent haste" (Earle 1973: 262), even though it lasts for many years. Similarly, details concerning the children of both protagonists are shrouded in silence, since they do not contribute to the image of a self-governing and unscrupulous woman.[78]

---

[78] Earle (1973) comments on the narrative function of children in *Moll Flanders*: "The children who are born to Roxana and Moll are treated in an abominable way, farmed out, killed

The selective representation of time in the two narratives may give rise to certain narrative inconsistencies. For example, since Moll strives to depict the horror of discovering that she is a wife to her own brother, she speaks elaborately about her anxiety and hesitation to reveal the truth. As a consequence, her incestuous relationship is prolonged by another three years, which may rightly be perceived as a highly unrealistic period of time.[79]

IV.4. Between Experience and Inexperience

Another inherent paradox of confession lies in the fact that it combines the inexperience of the doer and the experience of the speaker. The protagonists have "a short memory": they live "from incident to incident." However, both have "a minute recollection of distant events" (Rogers 1974: 264). They take part in the story they narrate, hence the tension between their knowledge and naivety.

Both the Amorous Woman and Moll tell their stories retrospectively. As a consequence, they should be "significantly wiser or shrewder" (Bell 1985: 162) than they were at the time of the events. Nonetheless, they sometimes tend to forget the wisdom they gained with time and they become again the inexperienced young women they used to be.

Saikaku's heroine notices at the beginning of her confessional narrative:

> In my young days I had no intention of entering on this path. Howbeit, I took a fancy to the manners of these young girls and used to go all the way from Uji to study their fashionable art. I found that I had a natural talent for dancing (AW 128).

Here she emphasises her innocence, while at the same time showing her propensity for wanton behaviour.

Having made this comment, the Amorous Woman proceeds to describe various stages in her career which are distinguished by the degree of the intensity of her erotic life. Interestingly, whenever she decides to abandon her promiscuous behaviour, she claims to return, almost miraculously, to her original state of innocence, which – of course – does not last long. She

---

off or forgotten, never brought up but occasionally brought in to provide some sort of dramatic tension" (262).

[79] "Despite this horror, Moll conceals her discovery for three years – a period more appropriate to a leisurely romance than to a dynamic, realistic novel" (Bell 1985: 163).

says at one point: "I had cast aside all wanton ways and was living in perfect innocence when one day I received a visit from a young gentleman, who was then at the height of his virile charms" (AW 154). Obviously, the Amorous Woman is neither able nor eager to learn from her previous experience, as she time and again falls into the snare of her own passions.

Unlike the Amorous Woman, Moll Flanders attempts to present her story as a process of gaining experience.[80] She insists on her immaturity from the outset: "I had no Policy in all this; you may easily see it was all Nature; but it was joined with so much Innocence and so much Passion that, in short, it set the good Motherly Creature a-weeping too" (MF 12). Furthermore, Moll occasionally focuses on her newly gained experience. For example, when her Bath lover decides to leave her, she realises: "I found by experience, that to be Friendless is the worst Condition, next to being in want that a Woman can be reduc'd to" (MF 128). In this manner, she leads the reader through the subsequent stages in her life.

Moll has succeeded in persuading a number of critics about her gradual progress "from youth to age, innocence to experience, and poverty to wealth" (Sutherland 1971: 170). Equally, she may be said to have obtained through various episodes in her life the awareness of a moral code and the ability to repent for her trespasses. Finally, her narrative may be regarded as a process of acquiring independence and "relative freedom" (Richetti 1975: 139).

However, it cannot be overlooked that Moll is frequently inconsistent in presenting her own moral, psychological or social development. Despite all her claims to the contrary, she is very often immune to experience, as she repeats the same mistakes.[81] Of course, she is even less able to learn from the experience of other characters. For example, although she draws a parallel between her own lot and the lives of other thieves who end up in Newgate,[82]

---

[80] Sutherland (1971) interprets Moll's development as follows: "In stories like Moll Flanders and Colonel Jack there is a sort of progress from youth to age, innocence to experience, poverty to wealth and so on. There is also some correlation between character and circumstance, and there is to some extent a development of character, although any advance towards moral virtue is usually accompanied by a good deal of compromise and backsliding" (170).

[81] Starr (1971) even observes that "if Moll is in some way the product of sociological and psychological conditioning, in other ways she is quite untouched by experience, a free spirit whom no pitch can defile" (ix).

[82] At one point Moll cries in despair: "Lord, *said* I, what am I now? a Thief! Why, I shall be taken next time, and be carried to *Newgate* and be Try'd for my Life!" (MF 192). After her accomplices in crime are sent to Newgate she confesses: "I Went frequently to see them, and

it does not prevent her from committing further crimes. Some critics explain Moll's behaviour by referring to her pride and obstinacy as she considers herself "superior, more careful, more dexterous, more intelligent than her criminal cohorts" (Krier 1971: 404). In this respect, Moll appears to be not all that dissimilar from Saikaku's Amorous Woman.

Therefore, the stories told by both the Amorous Woman and Moll oscillate between the experience and the inexperience of their protagonists. They also contain a tinge of hypocrisy, as the narrators attempt to emphasise their innocence in order to achieve their own means.[83] In this way, Saikaku's heroine presents herself as a woman of untamed passion and inconstant heart. This image was especially attractive for the readers in the "floating world" of the late seventeenth-century Japan. The swift changes in her attitude frequently become an important source of situational humour. Moll Flanders, while creating an illusion of her own self-development, is able not only to "cheer herself up in the past and present" (Novak 1970: 359), but also to vitalise her story – the story of an inconsistent woman wanting to appeal to the readers' sympathy.

IV.5. Possibility of Irony

The term "irony" is often avoided by Ihara Saikaku's critics as his works are considered to have "no unified narrative point of view [which] would not be able to register an ironic disruption" (Johnson 2001: 340). Instead, such terms as *chaka suru* ("to poke fun at"), *gyakuten suru* ("to invert, reverse") are used (Johnson 2001: 340). However, the discrepancy between experience of the narrator and the inexperience of the protagonist in a work adopting a form of confession inevitably evokes the question of irony, which in its most primary sense is understood as a gap between the reality and the appearance as first meant by the Greek word *eiron* (Baldick 2001: 76) or a "mode of speech in which the meaning is contrary to the words" (Makaryk 1993: 572). This primary meaning then was developed into a more com-

---

Condole with them, expecting that it would be my turn next; but the place gave me so much Horror, reflecting that it was the place of my unhappy birth, and of my Mother's Misfortunes, and that I could not bear it, so I was forced to leave off going to see them" (MF 204).

[83] Goldknopf (1969) focuses on Moll's narrative dishonesty, saying that "there is, then, a fundamental confessional duplicity in the novel, a duplicity which we, of course, share and enjoy. The tincture of hypocrisy in Moll's confession brightens the authenticity of their substance: that hypocrisy is also 'true to life'" (21).

plex definition of irony as "an attitude of detachment and sophistication and a tendency to perceive life in terms of the incongruities that occur between appearances and reality" (*Encyclopedia of Literature* 331).

A fictional confession suggests various levels of possible irony between the words and the knowledge of the characters, the narrator and the author of the book, whose presence may be presumed and detected not only in the preface but also throughout the whole work.[84] There are numerous examples of dramatic irony, "in which the audience knows more about a character's situation than the character does" (Baldick 2001: 130), both in *The Life of an Amorous Woman* and in *Moll Flanders*. In Saikaku's work, many a time the characters in one scene differ in their understanding of the situation and the discrepancy in their knowledge has a comic effect.

In most cases, Saikaku exposes the difference between the Amorous Woman and the ways in which she is perceived by others. As Hibbett notices, Saikaku "does not hesitate to destroy the continuity of his tale by digressing, by commenting on generalities wherever he cares to" (Hibbett 1957: 64). Apart from general comments interwoven in the narration, some of which may be attributed to Saikaku himself, there are numerous moments showing the discrepancy between the knowledge of the persona who narrates and the one who is narrated. Furthermore, there is a noticeable gap between the attitude of the Amorous Woman and that of other characters. Here is how she comments upon reactions to her promiscuous behaviour:

> Because I was only twelve years old at the time, people were disposed to pass over my fault; indeed they could hardly believe such an intrigue possible for one of my tender years. I myself could not help being amused at their feelings (AW 125).

From the distance of the years that passed she recalls how she used to indulge in other people's gullibility. Later, she even indicates how she was able to conveniently profit from it:

> This good couple, seeing in me a mere child whose appetites must as yet be unawakened, had me couch between them where they slept. As I lay there, a witness to their amorous intercourse, I was beset by strange feelings (AW 129).

As a consequence, the Amorous Woman seduces the "good" husband irrespective of his wife sleeping in the same bed.

---

[84] Darmosh (1988) speaks about "the triple levels of the first-person narrative,' as he distinguishes 'Moll as character, Moll as narrator, Defoe as novelist" (153).

In Saikaku's case, irony is used in a context of parody, as the Buddhist confession is gradually transformed into a burlesque (Hibbett 1957: 57–73). In Defoe's novel, which uses confession primarily to authenticate Moll's testimony, the dramatic irony is more intricate. When Moll as a child associates the word "gentlewoman" merely with the ability to provide for oneself in any possible way, lawful or illicit, she unintentionally foreshadows her future career as a "whore" and a "thief".[85] Additionally, Defoe seems to shift the meaning of the word "gentle," which is used throughout the novel to also denote dishonesty and deceit.[86] For example, the elder brother is frequently referred to as a "gentleman" with "Levity enough to do an ill natur'd thing' and 'too much judgment of things to pay too dear for his Pleasures" (MF 19). It is the elder brother who finally rejects Moll and advises her to marry Robin, claiming that she should "not stand in the way of [her] own Safety and Prosperity" (MF 55). And again Moll twists the meaning of his words to adjust it to her own means later in the novel.[87]

Dramatic irony is evident in the scene where Moll's mother-in-law speaks unguardedly about her past and is thereby revealed to be Moll's real mother. She discloses her secrets, "how she had fallen into very ill Company in *London* in her young Days" (MF 87). Her story is gradually recognised by Moll as that of her own mother: "I began to be very uneasy; but coming to one Particular that requir'd telling her Name, I thought I should have sunk

---

[85] Ian Watt (1957) perceives the dramatic irony in how Moll regards one of her "leisured but scandalous neighbours" as her ideal of "gentlewomanly life." Moreover, he claims that "[w]e can be certain that the irony is conscious because its tenor is supported by Defoe's other writings, which often show a somewhat rancorous spirit towards the failure of the gentry to provide proper models of conduct" (121).

[86] Novak (1983) comments on the use of word-play in *Moll Flanders*: "Occasionally Defoe will use word-play to underscore the ambiguity of a situation. Moll is apt at puns and the reader has to question Moll's surface accounts on these occasions. Sometimes the story itself has its ironies" (61). Bell (1985) focuses on the ironic use of the word "gentlewoman" in *Moll Flanders*: "First of all, there is the unwitting revelation that Moll's conception of reality is limited, in that her paragon is at best a humble lace-mender. Secondly, there is the further disconcerting news that she is not even a lace-mender, but a bawd of some sort, and so not a plausible 'gentlewoman' at all. And thirdly, there is the organising irony that Moll does indeed become such a 'Gentlewoman' eventually, though she cannot know that at the moment of original utterance" (159–160).

[87] Birdsall (1985) comments on the ironic meaning of the elder brother's advice: "The statement aptly summarizes the irony of Moll's existence: complacency, yes – but caution as well" (100).

down in the place" (MF 88). The juxtaposition of Moll's tragic discovery and the woman's frank confession has the effect of irony.

Apart from the dramatic irony in both novels, both women often make sarcastic comments in response to the circumstances they find themselves in. The Amorous Woman, as a mistress in a Buddhist monastery, speaks directly about the lustful and hypocritical life of the monks: "In the course of time I urged this one religion on temples of all the eight sects, and I may say that I never found a single priest who was not ready to slash his rosary" (AW 149). She refers to her sexual activity as "this one religion" while exposing the weaknesses of the monks.

For her part, Moll Flanders emphatically quotes the words of one of the Colchester sisters:

> [T]he Market is against our Sex just now; and if a young Woman have Beauty, Birth, Breeding, Wit, Sense, Manners, Modesty, and all these to an Extreme, yet if she have not Money, she's no Body, she had as good want them all for nothing but Money now recommends a Woman; the Men play the Game all into their own Hands (MF 20).[88]

The fact that the speaker is a wealthy and well-educated woman who addresses her message both to her brother and to Moll – a chambermaid – contributes to the implicit irony.

Moreover, there are numerous descriptions of the youthful Moll presented from a detached and thus ironic point of view. Many of them refer to Moll's response to the advances made by the elder brother. They suggest her unwillingness to resist the man's charm and passion: "I struggl'd to get away, and yet did it but faintly neither, and he held me fast, and still Kiss'd me, till he was almost out of Breath" (MF 22).[89] At times Moll is also explicitly ironic about her own vanity:

> I had with all these the common Vanity of my Sex, (*viz.*) That being really taken for very Handsome, or, if you please, for a great Beauty, I very well knew it, and had as good an Opinion of myself as anybody else could have of me (MF 19).[90]

---

[88] This exemplifies Moll's "editorial" role to present the reader with her ideas "concerning the position of the female in the society" (Krier 1971: 401).

[89] Watt (1967) notices that the scenes of Moll's seduction present a "consistently realistic amalgam of coquetry, covetousness, lust and genuine love in Moll's youthful consciousness: and the narrative voice is therefore ironic in the sense that it is a detached observer of a human folly" (120).

[90] Moll's comment illustrates what Bell (1985) calls a "separation of agent and narrator" (173).

There is enough of a sense of detachment in Moll's comment to enable an ironic reading of this passage.

Of course, although there are examples of what may be interpreted as irony in the two novels, many of them are far from being unambiguous. For example, the fact that the Amorous Woman indulges in her romances to an extent which may inflame rather than warn her male listeners may be considered either ironic or not. Similarly, the passage where Moll justifies her act of robbing a child of a precious necklace "of Gold Beads" (MF 194) by implicating the child's inattentive parents and nanny may be interpreted as either an example of irony of character or a possibly true-to-life reaction.[91]

The interpretation of narrative incongruities in *The Life of an Amorous Woman* and *Moll Flanders* is also complicated by the fact that modern readers tend to read these novels within categories that were entirely irrelevant in the times of Saikaku and Defoe. It is, therefore, possible that those narrative discrepancies may "not have answers or, for that matter, that they are [not] actually riddles at all" (Darmosh 1988: 159). Of course, it does not mean that the attempts to interpret what we today perceive as irony in Saikaku's or Defoe's writings have to be fruitless, only that they should be made cautiously and prudently.

IV.6. Confession and Modern Narrative

The analysis of *Moll Flanders* and *The Life of an Amorous Woman* poses further questions regarding not only the influence of literary traditions on the two works but also the relationship between the mode of confession and the development of modern narratives. Both questions are intricately related, as may be seen in Katō Shūichi's comment:

> Few will dispute that the two great mainstreams of tradition in Japanese literature are formed by the short poems that begin with the *Manyōshū* and by the prose diary form that begins with the *Kagerō no Nikki* and extends to the diaries and belles lettres of the Edo period. What happened to these two great currents following the Meiji Restoration?... (Katō 1971: 186).

---

[91] Birdsall (1985) believes that Moll's devious reasoning proves that "for Moll – and for Defoe – morality is a way of dealing with morality: it is a matter of self-interest" (91).

Katō focuses on the relationship between Japanese traditions of poetry and prose and Japanese modern literature and his words are recalled by Hijiya-Kirschnereit in her inspiring study of *shishōsetsu*, or Japanese modern narratives of self-revelation. Hijiya-Kirschnereit (1996) concludes that the "continuity of immanent structural principles of literary art" and a "cultural code" made it "possible for diary prose, and correspondingly shishōsetsu literature, to develop as it has" (298). She recognises that the origins of *shishōsetsu* are related to the fact that "the private and privatistic became a subject for literature" which made "the mainstream of *shizenshugi*" (the Japanese term for naturalism) shift "to confessional literature whose aesthetic value began to be judged according to the sincerity of the confession" (3). It is possible to say that the focus on the private, one of the characteristics of *shishōsetsu*, echoes Saikaku's choice of one individual as a narrator and protagonist in *The Life of an Amorous Woman*. Although Saikaku is not bound by the category of truthfulness in his narrative, he craftily uses it to involve and entertain his readers.

Moreover, as Miyoshi (1974) noticed, "the new fiction would attempt to deal with the ordinary experience of ordinary people and would be written in the colloquial language from the average person's moral perspective" (ix). Although the program of "the new fiction" in Japan is associated with Western influences, its anticipation may also be found in Saikaku's oeuvre with its focus on the everyday experience.

It has been widely recognised that *shishōsetsu* may be written either in the first- or third-person, as long as the author is identifiable with the protagonist. There is, however, a noticeable change from third- to first-person narratives occurring in Meiji Japan. According to Miyoshi (1974), this "free shift in the point of view, and even in the narrative mode, from the third-person novel to the first-person diary, confession or letter" is one of the characteristics of Japanese modern novelists, including Futabatei Shimei, Natsume Sōseki, Shiga Naoya and Dazai Osamu (x).

In fact, it is not so much the first-person narration but rather a noticeable shift to a consistent point of view in fictional narratives that marks the beginning of modern novel in Japan, juxtaposed with *monogatari* and *otogizōshi*, in which the change of narrative perspective was common. Fowler (1988) explains the phenomenon by "the virtual absence in classical Japanese of pronouns, which would serve to identify characters plainly and distinguish them from the narrator, as well as the absence of clear diacritical and grammatical demarcations between the 'framing' discourse and the 'framed' story" (30).[92]

Although the confessional mode creates an interesting link between *shishōsetsu* and Saikaku's narration in *The Life of an Amorous Woman*, it would be highly difficult to argue that the work anticipates this particular convention of fiction developed in Meiji Japan. Contrary to *shishōsetsu*, Saikaku's stories are primarily fabrications, much as he liked to incorporate common gossip and refer to the events that truly happened (this strategy is also used in a number of his other works, including *Kōshoku Gonin Onna*). Saikaku's use of confession in order to validate the fabricated story is closer to *shōsetsu* (rather than *shishōsetsu*) as understood by Masao Miyoshi:

> [R]ather than a "credible fabrication which is yet constantly held up as false," the *shosetsu* is an incredible fabrication that is nonetheless constantly held up as truthful. Art is hidden, while honesty and sincerity are displayed. Distance is removed, while immediacy is ostensive.... The *shosetsu* is thus an art that refuses to acknowledge art (Miyoshi 1983: 233; Fowler 1988: 64).

It is Saikaku's use of *ukiyozōshi* tradition that enhanced his artistry in the field of fiction-writing. His works remain one of the best examples of Edo-period *kanazōshi*, "most important in the history of Japanese literature as a transitional form, bridging the gap between the medieval romance and the modern novel" (Lane 1957: 699). However it is Saikaku's use of confessional mode in *The Life of an Amorous Woman* (echoing the *zange* convention and the *nikki* tradition), which encouraged his use of a more consistent point of view, a characteristic trait of Japanese modern novel. This choice of narrative perspective marks one of the three important junctures in the process of establishing "cultural and personal selfhood" in Japan (Washburn 1995: 8).

The tradition of *nikki* and *nikki* literature in Japan is incomparably longer and richer than anywhere else but in England diaries, letters and essayistic notes were also incorporated into modern narratives. It appears that the writers of autobiographies were not only self-conscious but also acutely aware of the existing traditions, as is indicated in *A True Relation of My Birth,*

---

[92] In Japan, the story was most commonly narrated "from within." Fowler (1988) juxtaposes this tendency with the omniscient narration in western narratives: "In the classical western novel, from Fielding to Fowles, the narrator's omniscient perspective is validated solely by the novel's internal consistency; the narrator need not be situated vis-à-vis the characters in any concrete relationship, since s/he commands a suprahuman authority" (30).

Breeding, and Life (1656) by Margaret Cavendish (2000): "my Readers will not think me vain for writing my life, since there have been many that have done the like, as *Caesar*, *Ovid*, and many more, both men and women, and I know no reason I may not do it as well as they" (63).

Peter Heehs indicates that "by the end of the eighteenth century, the practice of keeping diaries was widespread in British society, so much so that it found its way into fiction" (91). Defoe explored it in *Robinson Crusoe* and in the *Journal of the Plague Year*, which proves that fiction at the time was widely influenced by confessional writings. Furthermore, fifty years after the publication of Defoe's *Moll Flanders*, Jean-Jacques Rousseau's *Confessions* were first printed – although the work was completed already in 1769 – and influenced the Romantic writers, such as William Wordsworth and Thomas Penson De Quincey.

The eighteenth century in England thus presents itself as a time when individuality was passionately explored in narration. It is even possible to argue that the use of confession and other (auto)biographical modes "with their richly detailed texture and their evocations of the mystery of personality," encouraged "the possibilities for verbal interpretation of human nature in its particularities" (Spacks 2006: 281). The novelty (or novel-like quality) of Defoe lies not only in "returning to some of the narrative forms and conventions" that he craftily adapted, but also – as Mullan names it – in "new 'voyages'" (259). Defoe travelled by the power of his imagination to distant lands, as Mullan vividly illustrates in his comparative reading of *Robinson Crusoe* and Swift's *Gulliver's Travels*. He also started a journey to the depth of human personality and his use of human experience was to be later developed in the eighteenth century novels of consciousness, exemplified by Jane Austen's *Emma* (Spacks 2006: 280).

Epilogue

The aim of this monograph was to analyse the use of confessional mode in two literary works by Daniel Defoe and Ihara Saikaku, which, although written within two different traditions, bear a number of narrative similarities. The fact that the two authors use confession as a mode of presenting reality indicates their interest in "what occurs in the individual mind under the impact of the temporal flux," which is a principle characteristic of the novel (Watt 1957: 22). It also proves the importance of the realism and reliability of the speaker – the two prerequisites of Lejeune's "autobiographical contract" – for the early modern novel. Confession, as one of the autobiographical modes, seems to suit well the expectations of the writers and the readers. Its use in fiction, however, also generates a number of problems.

In *The Life of an Amorous Woman* and *Moll Flanders* Saikaku and Defoe attempt to create trustworthy narrators and use realistic techniques of depiction while focusing on details and enumerating tangible objects. Simultaneously, they focus on what Richetti (1975) calls the "superior reality of the self" and try to appeal to their audiences, who all are an integral part of the confession (108). The coexistence of the confessors and their audiences, as well as the use of confession in writing fiction are inevitably a source of tension in the two works. The revelation of the narrators' past is accompanied by their conscious concealment of various details and by means of withholding certain information they succeed in attracting the attention of the readers, thus preparing a suitable setting for disclosure. Although they speak from the distance of time and place, they are entirely absorbed in their stories. When speaking about the past, they frequently use the *praesens historicum* to emphasise the immediacy of what is being described. Although they are experienced and advanced in years, they sometimes show naivety and ignorance characteristic of their childhood and youth.

The parallel reading of *Moll Flanders* and *The Life of an Amorous Woman* as narratives written in a mode of confession was also carried with an intention to shed light on the development of the novel in England and Japan. Both Daniel Defoe and Ihara Saikaku are often referred to as "realistic writers," and, although the term is elusive, it is commonly associated with the development of the novel which distinguishes itself from the previous traditions of epic and romance. In the novel, the interest is shifted from an idealised hero to a protagonist who is set in a more familiar context and who encounters captivating yet plausible adventures. Accordingly, Defoe's realism, which stems from "his vivid evocation of individuals" (Richetti 2008a: 121) may be compared to that of Saikaku.

The realism of Saikaku and Defoe is also dependent on their colourful depiction of the milieu and the characters as they "embraced the contradictions in life" and "shunned idealisation" (Danly 1981: 131). Saikaku wrote for entertainment but his prose "explores the nature of human existence in the floating world" (Deal 2005: 256) and his focus on a particular story and – in the case of *The Life of an Amorous Woman* – on one perspective testifies to the fact that "even premodern Japanese literatures attest to clear, if often decidedly different, expressions of subjective agency" (Fujii 1993: 12).

The vividness of Defoe's and Saikaku's styles is additionally related to their use of concrete images and specific places. The scenes they depict are rich in detail, with frequent references to the money and enumerations of items, such as clothing, furniture and decorations, which reflect the authors' background and personal interests and create a tangible reality to which readers might easily relate at the same time. The sense of immediacy is also achieved by the language they use, which is frequently colloquial and devoid of embellishment.

Both, Defoe and Saikaku, as they observe the surrounding reality with great attendance to details, simultaneously explore the previous literary traditions and genres. Defoe craftily uses elements of spiritual autobiography, criminal biography, diary and picaresque novel. Saikaku, who draws from *nikki* and *monogatari* conventions, moves to "witty burlesque and [a] satirical portrait of manners" of the time (Hibbett 1957: 63). The burlesque, which is accompanied by social criticism, is primarily used to entertain people.The flatness of Saikaku's characters may be said to result from this inclination for parody and burlesque, which is, however, an important stage in the development of realism, as it sharpens the sense of the surrounding reality. Although it is rather difficult to speak of psychological depth in the case of his protagonist, the use of confession in *The Life of an Amorous Woman* may be regarded as an important attempt to focus on one individual whose experiences and perspective (even if it is sometimes interrupted by an external narrator) sustain the narration and, as a consequence, as a crucial step in the development of the Japanese modern novel, which continues to use confession (or revelation) as a narrative mode.

Defoe's portrayal of Moll Flanders possibly has more depth than what Saikaku ever achieved in his *kōshoku mono*: "[t]he internalization of experience that he had already exploited in *Robinson Crusoe* was not put to use in creating a woman who questions everything about her society, from its institutions to the very language in which the usual exchanges of life are enacted" (Novak 1996: 57). Moll's reactions and emotions are no less important than the depiction of the outer reality: "the tension between an (eventually) controlled external world and a turbulent interiority is the imaginative heart of his realistic depiction of character" (Richetti 2008a: 132). The tension is further explained as something that constitutes "the modern individual":

> The modern individual, as Defoe imagines him and her, is not integrated into a community or a moral order. Rather, the social and the historical are encountered as shifting or mysterious realms that can in the best case offer opportunities for development. But more often for marginalized characters (or dispossessed like Moll and Roxana, disqualified as women from full agency), the socio-historical realm represents a massive, threatening opposition, a set of controlling or destructive forces that demand resistance or evasion for survival (Richetti 2008a: 133).

This dynamics between the outer and the inner realities anticipates one of the major themes of the modern novel.

In this monograph, both "novel" and "confession" were used as broad categories, which enabled – though not without reservations – a comparative reading of two works coming from two different cultural and sociological backgrounds. The attempts to define the terms in their literary and historical (biographical) contexts have brought to the forefront not only the narrative traditions in England and Japan but also the present-day understanding of what constitutes the modern novel. In this respect, the monograph possibly raises more questions than it answers. Nonetheless, while exploring what may be referred to as the dichotomy between English and Japanese narrative traditions, it also contributes, however insufficiently, to bridging the gap between "the Western novel" and the Japanese *shōsetsu*.

References

Aaron, Richard I (1952). *The Theory of Universals*. Oxford: Clarendon Press.

Aitken, Robert (2002). "Formal Practice: Buddhist or Christian." *Buddhist-Christian Studies*, Vol. 22, 63–76.

Alryyes, Ala (2006). "Description, the Novel and the Senses." *The Senses and Society*, Vol. 1. No. 1 (March), 53–70.

Alter, Robert (1964). *Rogue's Progress*. Harvard: Oxford University Press.

Baldick, Chris (2001). *The Concise Oxford Dictionary of Literary Terms*. Oxford, New York: Oxford University Press.

Barnouw, Jeffrey (2005). "Britain and European literature and thought." *The Cambridge History of English Literature 1660–1780*. Ed. John J. Richetti. Cambridge: Cambridge University Press, 423–444.

Bell, Ian A. (1985). "Narrators and Narrative in Defoe." *NOVEL: A Forum for Fiction*, Vol. 18, No. 2 (Winter), 154–172.

Berry, Mary Elizabeth (2006). *Japan in Print: Information and Nation in the Early Modern Period*. Berkley, Los Angeles: University of California Press.

Birdsall, Virginia Ogden (1985). *Defoe's Perpetual Seekers*. London: Blackwell.

Bishop, Jonathan (1952). "Knowledge, Action and Interpretation in Defoe's Novels." *Journal of the History of Ideas*, Vol. 13, No. 1 (January), 3–16.

Booth, Wayne C. (1974). *A Rethoric of Irony*. Chicago, London: University of Chicago Press.

Bourdaghs, Michael K. (2003). *The Dawn that never comes: Shimazaki Toson and Japanese nationalism*. New York, Chichester, West Sussex: Columbia University Press.

Brown, Homer O. (1971). "The Displaced Self in the Novels by Daniel Defoe." *ELH*, Vol. 38, No. 4. (December), 562–590.

Brown, Homer O. (1996). "The Institution of the English Novel: Defoe's Contribution." *NOVEL: A Forum on Fiction*, Vol. 29, No. 3 (Spring), 299–318.

Burton, Richard (1909). *Masters of the English Novel: A Study of Principles and Personalities*. New York: Henry Holt.

Cavendish, Margaret (2000). "A True Relation of My Birth, Breeding, and Life." *Paper Bodies: A Margaret Cavendish Reader*. Eds. Sylvia Bowerbank, Sara Mendelson. Peterborough, Ontario: Broadview Press, 41–63.

Chaber, Lois A. (1982). "Matriarchal Mirror: Woman and Capital in Moll Flanders." *PMLA*, Vol. 97, No. 2. (March), 212–226.

Chaiklin, Martha (2009). "Up in the Hair: Strands of Meaning in Women's. Ornamental Hair Accessories in Early Modern Japan." Eds. Marianne Hulsbosch, Elizabeth Bedford, Martha Chaiklin. Amsterdam: Amsterdam University Press.

Chandler, Frank Wadleigh (1907). *The Literature of Roguery*. Vol. 1. Boston: Houghton Mifflin.

Chevalley, Abel (1925). *The Modern English Novel*. New York: A.A. Knopf.

Childs, Margaret H. (1987). "The Influence of the Buddhist Practice of Sange on Literary Form: Revelatory Tales." *Japanese Journal of Religious Studies*, Vol. 14, No. 1, 53–66.

Coetzee, J.M. (1985). "Confession and Double Thoughts: Tolstoy, Rousseau, Dostoyevsky." *Comparative Literature*, Vo. 37, No. 3 (Summer), 193–232.

Connor, Rebecca Elisabeth (2004). *Women, Accounting, and Narrative: Keeping Books in Eighteenth-Century England*. New York: Routledge.

Cranston, Edwin A. (1969). *The Izumi Shikibu Diary. A Romance of the Heian Court*. Massachussetts: Cambridge.

Cuddon, John Anthony (1992). *The Penguin Dictionary of Literary Terms and Literary Theory*. London: Penguin.

Danly, Robert Lyons (1981). *In the Shade of Spring Leaves: The Life and Writings of Higuchi Ichiyo*. New Haven,. Conn.: Yale University Press.

Dannenberg, Hilary P. (2004). "A Poetics of Coincidence in Narrative Fiction." *Poetics Today*, 25.3, 399–436.

Danziger, Marlies K. (1962). "The Eighteenth-Century Novel: A Comparative Approach." *College English*, Vol. 23, No. 8 (May), 646–648.

Darmosh, Leopold Jr. (1988). "Myth and Fiction in *Robinson Crusoe*." *Daniel Defoe's Robinson*. Ed. Harold Bloom. New York: Chelsea House, 84–85.

David Goldknopf (1969). "The Confessional Increment: A New Look at the I-Narrator." *The Journal of Aesthetics and Art Criticism*, Vol. 28, No. 1 (Autumn), 13–21.

Davis, Lennard J. (1980). "Wicked Actions and Feigned Words: Criminals, Criminality and the Early English Novel." *Yale French Studies*, No. 59, Rethinking History: Time, Myth and Writing, 106–118.

Davis, Lennard J. (1996). *Factual Fictions: The Origins of the English Novel*. Philadelphia.

De Visser, Marinus Willem (1935). *Ancient Buddhism in Japan*, The Netherlands: E.J. Brill.

Deal, William E. (2005). *Handbook to Life in Medieval and Early Modern Japan*. New York: Oxford University Press.

Defoe, Daniel (1969). *Life, Adventures and Pyracies of the Famous Captain Singleton*. London: Oxford University Press.

Defoe, Daniel (1971). *The Fortunes and Misfortunes of the Famous Moll Flanders*. London: Oxford University Press.

Dictionary of World Literature: Criticism, Forms, Technique (1943). Ed. Joseph T. Shipley. New York: Philosophical Library.

Dobrée, Bonamy (1959). *English Literature in the Early Eighteenth Century 1700–1740*. Oxford: Clarendon Press.

Dore, Ronald P. (1984). *Education in Tokugawa Japan*. London: The Athlone Press, Ann Arbor: Center for Japanese Studies, The University of Michigan.

Earle, Peter (1973). *The World of Defoe*. London: Weidenfeld and Nicolson.

Encyclopedia of Literature (1946). Ed. Joseph T. Shipley. New York: Philosophical Library.

Eubanks, Charlotte D. (2011). *Miracles of Book and Body. Buddhist Textual Culture and Medieval Japan*. Berkeley, Los Angeles, California: University of California Press.

Fludernik, Monika (2003). "Chronology, Time, Tense and Experientiality in Narrative." *Language and Literature*, Vol. 12, No. 2, 117–134.

Foster, James R. (1949). *History of the pre-Romantic Novel in England*. London: Oxford University Press.

Fowler, Edward (1988). *The Rhetoric of Confession: Shishosetsu in Early Twentieth-Century Japanese Fiction*. Berkeley, Los Angeles: University of California Press.

Fujii, James A. (1993). *Complicit Fictions. The Subject in the Modern Prose Narrative*. Berkley, Los Angeles, Oxford: University of California Press.

Fujimoto, Giichi (1999). *Saikaku yomigaeru*. Tokyo: NHK Ningendaigaku.

Gower, John (1889). *Tales of the Seven Deadly Sins: Being the Confessio Amantis*. London: Routledge.

Guillen, Claudio (1971). "Toward a Definition of a Picaresque." *Literature as System: Essays toward the Theory of Literary History*. Princeton: Princeton University Press.

Hamada, Kengi (1964). "Introduction." Ihara Saikaku. *The Life of an Amorous Man*. Trans. Hamada, Kengi. Rutland: Charles E. Tuttle Company, 5–8.

Hart, Francis R. (1970). "Notes for an Anatomy of Modern Autobiography." *New Literary History*, Vol. 1, No. 3, History and Fiction. (Spring), 485–511.

Heehs, Peter (2013). *Writing the Self: Diaries, Memoirs, and the History of the Self*. New York: Bloomsbury.

Hentzi, Gary (1991). "Holes in the Heart: Moll Flanders, Roxana, and "Agreeable Crime." *boundary 2*, Vol. 18, No. 1 (Spring), 174–200.

Hibbett, Howard (1952). *Saikaku as a Realist*. "Harvard Journal of Asiatic Studies." Vol. 15. No. 3/4 (Dec.), 408–418.

Hibbett, Howard (1957). *Saikaku and Burlesque Fiction*. "Harvard Journal of Asiatic Studies." Vol. 20, No. 1/2 (Jun.), 53–73.

Hibbett, Howard (1959). *The Floating World in Japanese Fiction*. New York: Oxford University Press.

Hibbett, Howard (1993). "Saikaku to Ningen no Kigeki." *Saikaku Bungaku no Miryoku*. Ed. Sanbyakunensaikenshōkai. Tokyo: Benseisha, 50–66.

Hijiya-Kirschnereit, Irmela (1996). *Rituals of Self-Revelation: Shishōsetsu as Literary Genre and Socio-Cultural Phenomenon*. Cambridge (Massachusetts), London: Harvard University Press.

Hindmarsh, D. Bruce (2005). *The Evangelical Conversion Narrative: Spiritual Autobiography in Early Modern England*. Oxford: Oxford University Press.

Hioki, Kazuko (2009). "Characteristics of Japanese Block Printed Books in the Edo Period: 1603–1867." *The Book and Paper Group Annual*, Vol. 28, 23–29.

Hiroshima, Susumu (1993). "Saikaku no nazo 20." *Saikaku hikkei*. Ed. Taniwaki Masachika. Tokyo: Gakutōsha, 151–169.

Horovitz, Irving Louis (1977). "Autobiography as a Presentation of Self for Social Immortality." *New Literary History*, Vol. 9, No. 1, Self-Confrontation and Moral Vision. (Autumn), 173–179.

Hühn, Peter (2001). "The Precarious Autopoiesis of Modern Selves: Daniel Defoe's *Moll Flanders* and Virginia Woolf's *The Waves*." *European Journal of English Studies*, Vol. 5, No. 3, 335–348.

Johnson, Jeffrey (2001). "Saikaku and the Narrative Turnabout." *Journal of Japanese Studies*, Vol. 27, No. 2 (Summer), 323–345.

Kamachi, Noriko. Hanchao Lu (1999). *Culture and Customs of Japan*. Westport: Greenwood Press.

Karatani, Kōjin (1993). *Origins of Modern Japanese Literature*. Trans. Brett De Bary. Durham, NC: Duke University Press.

Katō, Shūichi (1971). *Form, style, tradition: reflections on Japanese art and society*. Berkeley: University of California Press.

Katō, Shūichi (1980). *Nihon bungaku shi josetsu*, Vol. 2. Tokyo: Chikumashobō.

Katō, Shūichi (1997). *History of Japanese Literature: From the Man'yōshū to Modern Times*. London: Routledge.

Kearney, Richard (2001). *On Stories*. London: Routledge.

Keene, Donald (1971). *Appreciation of Japanese Culture*. Tokyo, New York, London: Kodansha International.

Keene, Donald (1995). *Modern Japanese Diaries: The Japanese at Home and Abroad As Revealed Through Their Diaries*. New York: Henry Holt.

Keene, Donald (1999). *Travelers of a Hundred Ages: The Japanese As Revealed Through 1,000 Years of Diaries* New York: Columbia University Press.

Keene, Donald (1999). *World Within Walls. Japanese Literature of the Pre-Modern Era 1600–1807*. New York: Columbia University Press.

Keene, Donald (2001). *"Realizm i nierzeczywistość w teatrze japońskim." Estetyka japońska I*. Ed. Krystyna Wilkoszewska. Kraków: Universitas.

Kibbie, Anne Louise (1995). "Monstrous Generation: The Birth of Capital in Defoe's *Moll Flanders* and *Roxana*," *PMLA* 110: 1023–1034.

Kim, He-Jin (1987). *Dogen Kigen. Mystical Realist*. Tucson: University of Arizona.

Koonce, Howard L. (1963). "Moll's Muddle: Defoe's Use of Irony." *ELH*, Vol. 30, No. 4 (December), 377–394.

Kordzińska-Nawrocka, Iwona (2010). *Ulotny świat ukiyo. Obraz kultury mieszczańskiej w twórczości Ihary Saikaku*. Warszawa: Wydawnictwa Uniwersyteu Warszawskiego.

Kornicki, Peter (1998). *The Book in Japan: A Cultural History from the Beginnings to the Nineteenth Century*. Leiden: Brill.

Krier, William J. (1971). "A Courtesy which Grants Integrity: A Literal Reading of Moll Flanders." *ELH*, Vol. 38, No. 3 (Sep.), 397–410.

Lane, Richard (1955). *Postwar Japanese Studies of the Novelist Saikaku*. "Harvard Journal of Asiatic Studies," Vol. 18, No. 1/2, 181–199.

Lane, Richard (1957). *The Beginnings of The Modern Japanese Novel: Kana-zōshi, 1600–1682*. "Harvard Journal of Asiatic Studies," Vol. 20, No. 3/4 (Dec.), 644–701.

Lane, Richard (1958). *Saikaku's Prose Works: a Bibliographical Study*. "Monumenta Nipponica," Vol. 14, No 1/2, 1–26.

Lane, Richard (1958–59). *Saikaku's Contemporaries and Followers: The Ukiyo-zoshi 1680–1780*. "Monumenta Nipponica," Vol. 14, No. 3/4 (Oct.–Jan.), 371–383.

Lane, Richard (1959). *Saikaku and Boccaccio. The Novella in Japan and Italy*. "Monumenta Nipponica," Vol. 15, No. 1/2 (Apr.–Jul.), 87–118.

Lane, Richard (1973). "Saikaku's *Five Women*." Ihara Saikaku. *Five Women Who Loved Love*. Trans. Theodore De Bary. Rutland: C.E. Tuttle, 231–263.

Lehmann, Paul (1953). "Autobiographies of the Middle Ages." *Transactions of the Royal Historical Society*, Vol. 3, 41–52.

Lejeune, Phillippe (1975). *Le pacte autobiographique*. Paris: Éditions du Seuil.

Lejeune, Phillippe (1989). "The Autobiographical Pact (Bis)." *On autobiography*. Minneapolis: The University of Minnesota Press, 119–137.

Magill, Frank Northern (2009). *Magill's Survey of World Literature. Revised Edition*. Vol. 2. Ed. Steven G. Kellman. Pasadena, California Hackensack, New Jersey: Salem Press, Inc.

Makaryk, Irena R. (1993). *Encyclopaedia of Contemporary Literary Theory*. Toronto, Buffalo, London: University of Toronto Press.

Mandel, Barrett John (1968). "The Autobiographer's Art." *The Journal of Aesthetics and Art Criticism*, Vol. 27, No. 2, 215–226.

Matsudo, Yukio (2000). "Protestant Character of Modern Buddhist Movement." *Buddhist-Christian Studies*, Vol. 20., 59–69.

Miller, J. Scott (2009). *Historical Dictionary of Modern Japanese Literature and Theatre*. Lanham, Md: Miller Scarecrow Press.

Miner, Earl (1968). "The Traditions and Forms of the Japanese Poetic Diary." *Pacific Coast Philology*, Vol. 3, 38–48.

Miyoshi, Masao (1974). *Accomplices of Silence. The Modern Japanese Novel*. Berkley, Los Angeles, London: University of California Press.

Miyoshi, Masao (1983). "Against the Native Grain: Reading the Japanese Novel in America." *Critical Issues in East Asian Literature: Report on an International Conference on East Asian Literature*. Seoul: International Cultural Society of Korea, 221–248.

Moretti, Laura (2012). "The Japanese early-modern publishing market unveiled: a survey of Edo-period booksellers' catalogues.'" *East Asian Publishing and Society*, 2:2, 199–308.

Mori, Osamu (1969). "Saikaku no buntai no jidaiteki igi." *Kokugo kokubun*, Vol. 24, No. 3, 173–180.

Morris, Ivan I. (1963). *Introduction*. Ihara Saikaku. *The Life of an Amorous Woman: And other Writings*. Trans. Ivan I. Morris. Norfolk: New Directions, 1–52.

Mostow, Joshua S. (2004). *At the House of Gathered Leaves. Shorter Biographical and Autobiographical Narratives from Japanese Court Literature*. Honolulu: University of Hawaii Press.

Mullan, John (1998). "Swift, Defoe and Narrative Forms." *The English Companion to English Literature, 1650–1740*. Ed. Steven N. Zwicker. Cambridge, New York, Melbourne: Cambridge University Press, 250–275.

Murasaki, Shikibu (1960). *The Tale of Genji: A Novel in Six Parts*. Transl. Arthur Waley. New York: Modern Library.

Needleman, Morriss H. Otis, William Bradley (1938). *A Survey-History of English Literature*. New York: Barnes & Noble.

Nenzi, Laura (2008). *Excursions in Identity: Travel and the Intersection of Place, Gender, and Status in Edo Japan*. Honolulu: Hawaii University Press.

Nishiyama, Matsunosuke (1997). *Edo Culture : Daily Life and Diversions in Urban Japan, 1600–1868*. Honolulu: University of Hawaii Press.

Novak, Maximillian E. (1963). *Defoe and the Nature of Man*. Oxford: Oxford University Press.

Novak, Maximillian E. (1970). "Defoe's Indifferent Monitor: The Complexity of Moll Flanders." *Eighteenth-Century Studies*, Vol. 3, No. 3. (Spring), 351–365.

Novak, Maximillian E. (1983). *Eighteenth Century English Literature*. The MacMillan Press.

Novak, Maximillian E. (1996). "Defoe as an Innovator of Fictional Form." *The Cambridge Companion to the Eighteenth Century Novel*. Ed. John J. Richetti. Cambridge: Cambridge University Press, 41–71.

Ogata, Tsutomu (1957). "Oranda Saikaku." Ed. Teruoka Yasutaka. *Saikaku*. Tokyo: Kadogawashoten, 273–282.

Olsen, Thomas Grant (2001). "Reading and Righting Moll Flanders." *Studies in English Literature 1500–1900*, 41, 3 (Summer), 467–481.

Paulson, Ronald (1967). *Satire and the Novel in the Eighteenth-Century England*. New Heaven & London: Yale University Press.

Piper, William Bowman (1969). "Moll Flanders as a Structure of Topics." *Studies in Literature, 1500–1900*, Vol. 9, No. 3. Restoration and Eighteenth Century. (Summer), 489–502.

Preston, John (1970). *The Created Self: The Reader's Role in Eighteenth-Century Fiction*. London: Heinemann.

Preus, J. Samuel (1991). "Secularizing Divination: Spiritual Biography and the Invention of the Novel." *Journal of the American Academy of Religion*, Vol. 59, No. 3 (Autumn), 441–466.

Rabin, Dana Y. (2003). "Searching for the Self in Eighteenth-Century English Criminal Trials, 1730–1800." *Eighteenth-Century Life*, 27.1, 85–106.

Richetti, John J. (1975). *Defoe's Narratives. Situation and structures.* Oxford: Clarendon Press.

Richetti, John J. (1996), "Introduction." *The Cambridge Companion to the Eighteenth Century Novel.* Ed. John J. Richetti. Cambridge: Cambrodge University Press, 1–8.

Richetti, John J. (1999). *The English Novel in History 1700–1780.* London: Routledge.

Richetti, John J. (2005). *The Life of Daniel Defoe: A Critical Biography.* Oxford: Blackwell Publishing.

Richetti, John J. (2008.a), "Defoe as Narrative Innovator." *The Cambridge Companion to Daniel Defoe.* Ed. John J. Richetti. Cambridge: Cambridge University Press, 121–138.

Richetti, John J. (2008.b), "Introduction." *The Cambridge Companion to Daniel Defoe.* Ed. John J. Richetti. Cambridge: Cambridge University Press, 1–4.

Rimer, Thomas J. (1978). *Modern Japanese Fictions and Its Traditions. An Introduction.* Princeton, New Jersey: Princeton University Press.

Rodrigues-Luis, Julio (1979). "Picaras: the Modal Approach to the Picaresque." *Comparative Literature*, Vol. 31, No. 1. (Winter), 32–46.

Rogers, Pat (1972). *Defoe: The Critical Heritage.* London: Routledge.

Rogers, Pat (1974). *The Augustan Vision.* London: Methuen.

Rogers, Pat (1978). *The Context of English Literature: the Eighteenth Century.* London: Methuen.

Rothschild, Jeffrey M. (1990). "Renaissance Voices Echoed: The Emergence of the Narrator in English Prose." *College English*, Vol. 52, No. 1. (January), 21–35.

Rubinger, Richard (2007). *Popular Literacy in Early Modern Japan.* Honolulu: University of Hawaii Press.

Ruch, Barbara (1994). "A Book of One's Own: The Gossamer Years; The Pillow Book; and The Confessions of Lady Nijō." *Masterworks of Asian Literature in Comparative Perspective: A Guide for Teaching.* Ed. Barbara Stoler Miller. Armonk, NY: M.E. Sharpe.

Saikaku, Ihara (1963). *The Life of an Amorous Woman: And other Writings.* Trans. Ivan I. Morris. Norfolk: New Directions.

Seigle, Segawa (1993). *Yoshiwara: The Glittering World of the Japanese Courtesan.* Honolulu: University of Hawaii Press.

Sherman, Stuart (2005). "Diary and Autobiography." *The Cambridge History of English Literature 1660–1780.* Ed. John J. Richetti. Cambridge: Cambridge University Press, 649–672.

Shimamura Hōgetsu (1975), "Saikaku ron." *Fūun shū.* Ed. Nihon kindai bungaku kan. Tokyo, 1–38.

Shimizu, Shigeru (1965). *Saikaku to shizenshugi ikō no bungaku.* "Kokubungaku kaishaku to kyōzai no kenkyū tokushū: Saikaku bungaku no tankyū," 10 (6). Tokyo: Gakutōsha, 49–54.

Skilton, David (1985). *Defoe to the Victorians: Two Centuries of the English Novel.* New York: Penguin Books.

Sources of Japanese Tradition. Vol II (2005). Ed. Wm. Theodore de Bary, Carol Gluck, Arthur E. Tiedemann. New York: Columbia University Press.

Spacks, Patricia Meyer (2006). *Novel Beginnings. Experiments in Eighteenth Century English Fiction*. New Haven, London: Yale University Press.

Starr, G.A. (1971). "Introduction." Daniel Defoe. *The Fortunes and Misfortunes of the Famous Moll Flanders*. London: Oxford University Press, iii–xxii.

Starr, G.A. (1974). "Defoe's Prose Style: The Language of Interpretation." *Modern Philology*. Vol. 71, No. 3. (February), 277–294.

Strange, Sallie Minter (1976). "Moll Flanders: A Good Calvinist." *The South Central Bulletin, Vol. 36, No. 4*. (Winter), 152–154.

Stubbs, David C. (1965). "Foreword." Ihara Saikaku. *This Scheming World*. Rutland: C.E. Tuttle, 7–16.

Sutherland, James (1938). *Defoe*. Philadelphia: J.B. Lippincott.

Sutherland, James (1971). *Daniel Defoe. A Critical Study*. Cambridge: Harvard University Press.

Suzuki, Daisetzu Teitaro (1935). *The Training of the Zen Buddhist Monk*. Kyoto: Eastern Buddhist Society.

Suzuki, Tomi (1996). *Narrating the Self:Fictions of Japanese Modernity*. Stanford, C.A.: Stanford University.

Teruoka, Yasutaka (1949). *Saikaku no Sekai*. Tokyo: Kimizusha.

Teruoka, Yasutaka (1957a). "Gendai no Me." *Saikaku*. Ed. Teruoka Yasutaka. Tokyo: Kadogawashoten, 332–338.

Teruoka, Yasutaka (1957b). *Saikaku Kenkyū Bunken Sōran*. "Kokubungaku." No. 6, 104–118.

The Bloomsbury Guide to English Literature (1995). Ed. Marion Wynne-Davies. London: Bloomsbury Publishing Place.

The Reader's Encyclopedia: An Encyclopedia of World Literature and the Arts (1948). Ed. William Rose Benét. New York: T. Y. Crowell.

Totman, Conrad D. (1995). *Early Modern Japan*. Berkeley: University of California Press.

Traganou, Jilly (2004). *The Tokaidō Road. Travelling and Representation in Edo and Meiji Japan*. New York, London: Routledge Curzon.

Tsubouchi, Shōyō (1960). "The Essence of the Novel." *Modern Japanese Literature: An Anthology*. Ed. Donald Keene. New York: Grove Press.

Ueda, Akinari (1974). *Ugetsu Monogatari: Tales of Moonlight and Rain: A Complete English Version of the Eighteenth-Century Japanese Collection of Tales of the Supernatural*. Ed. Leon M. Zolbrod. Vancouver, B.C.: University of British Columbia.

Uesaka, Ayaka. Murakami, Masakatsu (2014). *Verifying the authorship of Saikaku Ihara's work in early modern Japanese literature; a quantitative approach*. "Literary and Linguist Computing", http://dx.doi.org/10.1093/llc/fqu049 (accessed 30.01.2015).

Van Ghent, Dorothy (1961). *The English Novel: Form and Function*. New York.

Warner, William B. (2011). "Definitions of the Novel." *The Encyclopedia of the Novel*. Vol. 1. Ed. Peter Melville Logan. Malden, MA: Wiley-Blackwell, 224–233.

Washburn, Dennis C. (1995). *The Dilemma of the Modern in Japanese Fiction*. New Haven: Yale University Press.

Watt, Ian (1949). "The Naming of Characters in Defoe, Richardson and Fielding." *The Review of English Studies*, Vol. 25, No. 100. (October), 322–338.

Watt, Ian (1957). *The Rise of the Novel: Studies in Defoe, Richardson, and Fielding*. Berkeley: University of California Press.

Watt, Ian (1967). "The Recent Critical Fortunes of Moll Flanders." *Eighteenth-Century Studies*, Vol. 1, No. 1 (Autumn), 109–126.

Watt, Ian (1968). "Serious Reflections on 'Rise on the Novel'." *NOVEL: A Forum on Fiction*, Vol. 1, No. 3. (Spring), 205–218.

Watt, Ian (1988). "Individualism and the Novel." *Daniel Defoe's Robinson*. Ed. Harold Bloom. New York: Chelsea House, 11–41.

Weinberg, Bernard (1937). *French Realism: the Critical Reaction 1830–1870*. New York, London: The Modern Language Association of America.

Willey, Machiko M. (2004). *The Two Social Critics Daniel Defoe and Ihara Saikaku. A Comparative Study of* The Fortunes and Misfortunes of the Famous Moll Flanders *and* The Life of an Amorous Woman. Albuquerque: University of New Mexico Press.

Wilson, Frank Percy (1960). *Seventeenth Century Prose. Five Lectures*. Berkley, Los Angeles: University of California Press.

Yamashita, Itsukai (1966). "Oranda Saikaku." *Kokubungaku kaishaku to kyōzai no kenkyū tokushū: Saikaku bungaku no tankyū*. Tokio: Gakutōsha, 25–31.

Zwicker, Jonathan E. (2011). *"Japan." The Encyclopedia of the Novel*. Vol. 1. Ed. Peter Melville Logan. Malden, MA: Wiley-Blackwell, 439–449.

Annex

I. Daniel Defoe's Selected Works

An Essay Upon Projects (1697)
The True-Born Englishman: A Satyr (1701)
The Shortest Way with the Dissenters (1702)
Hymn to the Pillory (1703)
The Storm (1704)
The Consolidator or, Memoirs of Sundry Transactions from the World in the Moon (1705)
Atlantis Major (1711)
The Family Instructor (1715)
Memoirs of the Church of Scotland (1717)
Robinson Crusoe (1719)
The Farther Adventures of Robinson Crusoe (1719)
Captain Singleton (1720)
Memoirs of a Cavalier (1720)
Serious Reflections of Robinson Crusoe (1720)
A Journal of the Plague Year (1722)
Colonel Jack (1722)
Moll Flanders (1722)
Roxana: The Fortunate Mistress (1724)
The History Of The Remarkable Life of John Sheppard (1724)
A Narrative Of All The Robberies, Escapes, &c. of John Sheppard (1724)
A Tour Thro' The Whole Island of Great Britain, Divided into Circuits or Journies (1724–1727)
The Pirate Gow (1725)
The Political History of the Devil (1726)
The Complete English Tradesman (1726)
An Essay Upon Literature (1726)
Mere Nature Delineated (1726)
Conjugal Lewdness (1727)
A Plan of the English Commerce (1728)

112

II. Ihara Saikaku's Selected Works[93]

Kōshoku Ichidai Otoko 好色一代男 (The Life of an Amorous Man, 1682)
Kōshoku Nidai Otoko: Nanshoku Ōkagami 好色二代男 諸艶大鏡 (The Great Mirror of Beauties: Son of an Amorous Man, 1684)
Saikaku Shokoku Hanashi 西鶴諸国はなし (Saikaku's Tales from Various Provinces, 1685)
Kōshoku Gonin Onna 好色五人女 (Five Amorous Women, 1686)
Kōshoku Ichidai Onna 好色一代女 (The Life of an Amorous Woman, 1686)
Honchō Nijū Fukō 本朝二十不孝 (Twenty Cases of Unfilial Children, 1686)
Nanshoku Ōkagami 男色大鑑 (The Great Mirror of Male Love, 1687)
Budō Denraiki 武道伝来記 (Transmission of the Martial Arts, 1687)
Futokoro Suzuri 懐硯 (Inkstone in One's Bosom, 1887)
Shin Kashō Ki 新可笑記 (New Humorous Records, 1688)
Kōshoku Seisuiki 好色盛衰記 (Rise and Fall of Amorous Desire, 1688)
Arashi wa mujyō monogatari 嵐は無常物語 (Tale of Arashi, 1688)
Buke Giri Monogatari 武家義理物語 (Tales of Samurai Honor, 1688)
Nihon Eitai Gura 日本永代蔵 (The Eternal Storehouse of Japan, 1688)
Irozato Mitokoro Setai 色里三所世帯 (Three Noteworthy Sexual Situations, 1688)
Honchō Ōin Hiji 本朝桜陰比事 (Japanese Trials in the Shade of a Cherry, 1689)
Seken Munezan'yō 胸算用 (Reckonings that Carry Men Through the World, 1692)
Saikaku Oki Miyage 西鶴置土産 (A Present Left by Saikaku, 1693)
Ukiyo Eiga Ichidai Otoko 浮世栄花一代男 (The Man Who Flourished in the Floating World, 1693)
Saikaku Oridome 西鶴織留 (Some Final Words of Advice, 1694)
Saikaku Zoku Tsurezure 西鶴俗つれづれ (Saikaku's Miscellany, Continued, 1695)
Yorozu no Fumihōgu 万の文反古 (Plenty of Unnecessary Letters, 1696)
Saikaku Nagori no Tomo 西鶴名残の友 (A Companion to Remember Saikaku, 1699)

---

[93] The authorship of the numerous works attributed to Ihara Saikaku is an important research subject. The authorship is often not stated but based on the textual evidence (Lane 1958: 1–26). This list is based on the research by Uesaka and Murakami.

Index

TECHNICAL EDITOR
Anna Poinc-Chrabąszcz

PROOFREADER
Barbara Rydzewska

LANGUAGE REVISION
Keith Horechka

TYPESETTER
Katarzyna Mróz-Jaskuła

Jagiellonian University Press
Editorial Offices: Michałowskiego St. 9/2, 31-126 Kraków
Phone: +48 12 663 23 81, +48 12 663 23 82, Fax: +48 12 663 23 83